D0725536

"Exploring this tens

Wait...what? Jack thought Viv was about to bring up the chemistry between them? He clearly thought of her in that way or this wouldn't be an issue.

"I was—"

"I don't like tension in my work space."

"And you think there's a problem between us?"

Why was her whisper suddenly husky like some seductress? She certainly wasn't trying to seduce him. Not that she'd mind.

"I think you drive me out of my mind." Jack took a half step closer. "I blame myself for my thoughts, but I blame you for making me want things I have no business wanting."

"I'm not trying to do anything to you. I'm attracted to you, but I know you're my boss and that's a line we can't cross, even if you were interested in me that way."

Jack muttered a curse, took a step forward and had her pinned between his hard chest and the wall.

"*If* I was interested?" he repeated with a laugh of disbelief. "Do I look like a man who isn't interested, Viv?"

* * *

*The Heir's Unexpected Baby* is part of Harlequin Desire's #1 bestselling series, Billionaires and Babies: Powerful men...wrapped around their babies' little fingers.

Dear Reader,

Welcome to the final Mafia Moguls book, which is also a Billionaires and Babies novel! I hope you've enjoyed the journey so far, because Jack and Viv have quite a few twists and turns in store for you— and the infamous O'Shea family.

These two characters came to me before the first book in this series was ever written. I knew Viv would heal my stubborn, widowed hero. I loved her strength, her determination and her sass from the beginning.

Jack heals Viv, as well. He's broken, but refused to face the reality until he's forced to—and that's when things get interesting. Poor Jack. He's fought for years not to fall for his assistant, but he can't deny the truth any longer.

I'm so excited to save them for the close of this series and truly believe you'll love watching them fall into each other. This was one of those books that really pulled my emotions from deep down. The path wasn't easy—for my characters or me—but we made it to the end! Thank you for coming along for the ride.

Happy reading,

*Jules*

# JULES BENNETT

---

# THE HEIR'S UNEXPECTED BABY

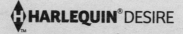

Recycling programs
for this product may
not exist in your area.

ISBN-13: 978-0-373-83824-0

The Heir's Unexpected Baby

**Printed in U.S.A.**

National bestselling author **Jules Bennett** has penned over forty contemporary romance novels. She lives in the Midwest with her high-school-sweetheart husband and their two kids. Jules can often be found on Twitter chatting with readers, and you can also connect with her via her website, julesbennett.com.

### Books by Jules Bennett

### Harlequin Desire

*What the Prince Wants*
*A Royal Amnesia Scandal*
*Maid for a Magnate*
*His Secret Baby Bombshell*

### *Mafia Moguls*

*Trapped with the Tycoon*
*From Friend to Fake Fiancé*
*Holiday Baby Scandal*
*The Heir's Unexpected Baby*

### Harlequin Special Edition

### *The St. Johns of Stonerock*

*Dr. Daddy's Perfect Christmas*
*The Fireman's Ready-Made Family*
*From Best Friend to Bride*

Visit her Author Profile page at Harlequin.com, or julesbennett.com, for more titles.

To everyone who has opened their homes and hearts to foster children...you are truly a blessing.

# One

"What are you doing here so early?"

Jack Carson brushed past Vivianna Smith and stepped into her apartment, trying like hell not to touch her. Or breathe in that familiar jasmine scent. Or think of how sexy she looked in that pale pink suit.

*Masochist.* That's all he could chalk this up to. But he had a mission, damn it, and he needed his assistant's help to pull it off.

Wouldn't life be so much easier if Viv were only his assistant? He'd avoided the unwanted attraction for four years, yet the longer she worked for him, the more difficult that was proving to be. And lately, he'd been having dreams. Okay, fine. Fantasies. And she starred in every single one of them.

How the hell could he even have these thoughts about her? It was flat-out wrong, not to mention unprofessional.

"I need you to use that charm of yours and get more information." He turned to face her as she closed the door to her apartment. "You're going to have to dig deeper into the Parkers' lives."

Clint and Lily Parker were a young couple who had been killed two months ago in a robbery gone wrong. The perpetrators set the Parkers' house on fire. The only survivor was a sweet infant named Katie…a baby Viv now fostered.

The burn in his chest was still crippling. Jack wasn't going down the baby path, not even in his mind. He admired Viv for reaching out and helping a child, as she had so many times over the years. But babies weren't for him. They never could be if he wanted to keep his heart intact.

"You're positive the O'Sheas had something to do with that crime?" Vivianna asked, moving around him to head down the hall.

With no option but to follow her swaying hips, he fell in right behind her. He was human, and a guy. Where else could he look but those hips? She always had on those damn body-hugging skirts…he believed she referred to them as pencil skirts. Those curves would be the death of him.

"I know they did," he confirmed.

The infamous O'Shea family of Boston was always slipping around the law, ignoring the basic rules of human decency. Jack's main focus in life was bringing cocky bastards like that down. Every time he went against those believing they were above the law, he saw the person who had killed his wife and unborn child…and still ran free.

The O'Sheas might run a polished high-society auction house known around the globe, but he knew they were no better than common criminals. And Jack was about to prove to this arrogant family who was in charge. He would bring them down in a spectacular show of justice. And his ticket was the woman who fueled his every fantasy.

A year ago, Jack had set up the perfect bogus background for Viv. She was working only part-time for the notorious family, but that's all he needed for her to gain intel.

The FBI had sought him out, needing someone with his experience and resources to infiltrate the O'Sheas. Since Jack was the best in the business of investigating, of course they needed him. That wasn't vanity, either, just a fact. Jack could get things done when others couldn't.

The millions he'd made hadn't rolled in by him sitting back and delegating responsibilities. He'd worked his ass off, throwing himself into his work and opening Carson Enterprises when he got home from Afghanistan ten years ago.

He'd returned to find that he'd lost his entire family while he'd been overseas. What else had there been to live for other than seeking justice anywhere he could?

Since he'd already made a fortune, he often turned

down jobs when they didn't appeal to him. But the O'Sheas were right in his wheelhouse. They had been in talks with the Parker couple about acquiring some of their antiques when the robbery happened. There wasn't a doubt in Jack's mind that this tight-lipped family knew what really went down that tragic night.

Viv went into the nursery. Heart clenching, Jack opted to wait in the hall—demons and all that.

He commended Viv for her love of children, the way she fostered with open arms. Over the time he'd known her, he'd seen her with various children, but never an infant. He couldn't get involved in any of that. The wounds he'd lived with for so long had never healed...probably never would.

Viv stepped back into the hall, Katie's head resting against her shoulder. "I need to drop her off at the sitter next door and get to work."

Viv was lucky that her next-door neighbor was a retired teacher and widow. She loved kids and took care of Viv's foster kids when she was working.

"I'm doing what I can, Jack." Her eyes held his and he hated how tired she looked. Beautiful, sexy as hell, but still tired. "They're already suspicious because of the missing data. If I press too hard, they'll know I'm not who I say I am."

Jack hadn't wanted to put her in this position. But he couldn't back down when he had a job to do. And that job wasn't staring at the V in her suit jacket as baby Katie tugged at the opening.

A flash of a white lacy bra taunted him, making him want to undo those few buttons to see if the lace...

*Damn it. Get a grip.*

She stepped forward, and Jack had to force himself to focus on her face. Which wasn't a hardship. Viv was part Native American. Her grandmother had been in the Sioux tribe, so Viv had inherited high cheekbones, long, dark hair and deep brown eyes. He'd seen more than one man do a double take her way...and each time, Jack had wanted to throat punch the stranger.

Guilt banded around his chest like a vise. He shouldn't be lusting after another woman. He'd had the love of his life; she was gone. Gone because he hadn't been there to protect her or their baby.

Getting drawn to Viv was just a by-product of working together for so long. She was the only woman he associated with, other than his housekeeper-slash-chef, Tilly. He admired Viv because she was strong, with an undertone of vulnerability. Add in her striking looks and perfectly shaped curves and it was only natural he be attracted to her. But he had to keep his emotions beneath the surface where he could control them.

"I'm on your side here," she told him with a soft smile, pulling him back to the moment. "Why don't you come over this evening and we can talk more."

"I have a conference call this evening with some clients in the UK."

Viv gave a slight nod. "Oh, okay. Then tomorrow? I'll make dinner and we can figure out our next step."

Dinner? With her and the baby? That all sounded so…domestic. He prided himself on keeping work in the office or in neutral territory. But he'd come here this morning to check on her…and he couldn't blame it all on work.

Damn it. The longer this case went on, the more protective he became—the more possessive.

"You can come to my place and I'll have my chef prepare something."

There. If Tilly was on hand, then maybe it wouldn't seem so family-like. Viv often fostered kids who had no place else to go. He had no idea why she'd never settled down and started a family of her own, when it was so obvious she loved caring for children. But that was none of his business. Just because they were associates didn't mean he had a right to pry into her life. Clearly, she didn't want to discuss such things or she would've brought them up.

"I can do tomorrow," she told him, her smile widening. "Katie and I would love to get out of the house. I get off work around four, so I'll pick her up and be right over."

Jack hadn't had her over with a child before. On the rare occasions he and Viv got together outside the office, it was usually just the two of them. In the past couple years, ever since he started really noticing Vivianna as more than his assistant, he'd tried to keep their social interactions to a minimum.

"Any requests?" he asked.

Did her gaze just dart to his lips? She couldn't look at him with those dark eyes as if she wanted…

No. It didn't matter what she wanted, or what he wanted for that matter. Their relationship was business only. Period.

"Um...no requests." She shook her head, offered a smile. "Whatever you have will be fine."

Jack rubbed his damp palms against his jeans. He needed to get out of here. Between that telling look she'd thrown him, the precious baby still sleeping in her little pink onesie and his lack of sleep from working, his mind was throwing all sorts of impossible scenarios at him.

Jack crossed to the door and gripped the doorknob. He glanced over his shoulder as Viv closed in behind him. "Be careful, Viv. I don't want you to take unnecessary risks."

She shifted the sleeping baby and tipped her head. "You've taught me how to look out for myself. I promise I'll be fine. See you tomorrow."

Jack paused, soaking in the sight of her in that prim little suit, holding the baby. Definitely time to go before he forgot she actually worked for him and took what he'd wanted for months. He didn't need any more heartache or distractions in his life.

It was finally four o'clock and Viv couldn't wait to get out of her office at O'Shea's and go see Jack. Ridiculous, this infatuation she had with her boss. Clichés were definitely not her thing, yet she'd be diving headfirst into his sheets if he gave her the green light.

Sad. She was a sad woman hoping her boss would

notice her. Like she had time for a torrid, steamy affair. She was caring for a child, an infant. There was nothing sexy about the haggard, overworked-mom look. But Viv would never give up fostering. She could still be a mother, yet not get too emotionally attached.

The heartache of knowing she'd never have her own children was somewhat pacified, yet the underlying hurt was never too far below the surface. But work kept her busy and her attentions focused elsewhere. It wasn't as if she didn't have a full load at the moment.

Viv started at O'Shea's part-time, which was perfect for her fostering schedule, not to mention that she still worked for Jack, as well. Being single, she had only a handful of people she could count on. Her parents were no longer around and she was an only child. She'd learned some time ago how to be independent, but even so, she needed some help when caring for a child and working outside the home.

Her quirky neighbor, Martha, was an adorable elderly lady who watched Katie most of the time, but when Viv was in a bind, she'd simply take Katie into the office. Well, her office with Jack.

Oh, she "worked" at O'Shea's, but that was only a cover created by Jack to get her on the inside, up close and personal. Her real employer was one sexy, rich investigator who couldn't move beyond his heartache to see there was still life out there.

If it wasn't work, he wasn't interested…which was the only reason he'd shown up so early at her house yesterday morning. The man had been through so much pain in his life, it was no wonder he was married to his job. He'd lost his mother when he'd been around nineteen, then he'd seen battle in war. His wife had been killed and he'd never known who his father was... Viv knew just enough details for her heart to break for him, but she wished he would try living again. She'd love to be the one to show him that not everything was harsh and cold...if he would only let her in.

Viv headed toward the back office of O'Shea's. Laney, the youngest O'Shea and the only female sibling, was out front dealing with a potential client. Since they had discovered some information had been leaked to the Feds, at least one member of the infamous family was here at all times...which made Viv's snooping a tad more difficult, considering she was here only about twenty hours per week.

Circling the antique desk that had been assigned to her in the office, she opened the top left drawer to find a pen. She wanted to jot down some items she needed to pick up from the store or she'd forget.

Katie was teething and the nights were getting longer and longer. Poor baby. She'd lost her parents and now she wasn't sleeping. Viv wanted to comfort the sweet girl while she was in her care.

All kids that came into Viv's home were precious, and they were all hard to say goodbye to. But Viv stayed strong for them. With this being her first baby, she worried how much more difficult it would be, both emotionally and logistically. She already had a demanding schedule, but she couldn't turn away this poor orphan who'd just lost both parents.

At the moment, Katie needed more pain reliever for her swollen gums, and Viv was out of nearly everything. Grocery shopping wasn't high on the priority list right now. Saving kids, helping Jack, trying to get Jack to notice her as more than a friend…would he ever? Her to-do list seemed to grow by the day.

Vivianna reached inside her desk for a pen and a slip of paper. She'd used this particular desk since coming here a year ago. During that time she'd earned the trust of the O'Sheas, and occasionally felt guilty about her act, but she wasn't naive. She'd heard the rumors around Boston. Anyone who delved into the art or auction world knew who the O'Sheas were. The terms *mafia* and *mob* seemed to follow them wherever they went.

Something brushed the top of her hand. Viv jerked back, bent down, but didn't see anything inside the drawer. If there was a spider in there tickling her skin there wouldn't be enough antibacterial gel to kill those horrendous germs.

She quickly reached back in for her pen and paper. And once again something brushed the back of her hand.

Viv reached for her cell phone and shone the light inside the drawer, fully expecting to see a family of hairy tarantulas.

When she bent down, she saw a sliver of paper sticking out…from the top of the drawer? Since Viv had used this desk for so long, she had no idea what that could be.

She listened. Laney and the client were still talking. Viv's desk sat in the corner, away from them, so the coast was clear. Pulling her chair over, she took a seat and bent to examine the underside of the desk. How had she not noticed anything before?

Gripping the paper between her thumb and index finger, she tugged slightly. When it eased out further, she noticed some cursive writing she couldn't identify. Pulling a bit more, she felt something give. Putting her phone inside the drawer to shine upward, she reached with both hands. The board was loose.

Viv pulled slightly, careful to not make too much noise, but Laney and the client were now laughing. Perfect.

The board was a bit of a struggle, but it came loose. And a small book fell into the drawer.

Viv stared, curious about where it had come from and who'd hidden it in the desk. She quickly grabbed her purse from the bottom drawer and slid the book inside. She'd have to look at it later.

Grocery list forgotten—she could worry about that later—Viv grabbed her things. She belted her wrap coat and quickly hoisted her purse up onto her shoulder as she headed out the back door. The bitter wind cut right through her, but she was anxious to get to her car.

Once she settled into her older model car, Viv turned on her heated seat, locked the doors and pulled the small leather-bound book from her purse.

It didn't take her long to realize she'd struck gold. The author of this journal was none other than the late Patrick O'Shea. The patriarch of the Boston family Jack was hell-bent on bringing down. The family she'd been infiltrating for a year.

As she skimmed the pages, she knew when she got to Jack's house he'd devour this thing. She couldn't wait to get this to him, to show him she was valuable and actually had something concrete they might be able to use.

She flipped another page, then froze as she read the entry. Her blood chilled as each word sank in. There was no skimming this one. In fact, she read it twice to make sure she wasn't seeing things.

Heart in her throat, she knew there was no way Jack could ever see this journal. Everything he'd wanted to bring down the family was here…including the fact that Jack was Patrick's illegitimate son.

# Two

Heels clicked on the hardwood, the echo growing louder as Viv approached. Jack came to his feet and turned toward the entryway of the patio room. He'd had his chef set up dinner out here so they could close all the French doors and have some privacy.

Jack sucked in a breath the second she came into view. The punch of lust to the gut was nothing new, though. More and more, when he saw her, she never failed to have a dramatic impact…an issue he'd have to deal with on his own.

Her pink suit jacket cut in at her narrow waist, the matching skirt fell just above her knee and her black heeled boots showcased just how long those legs truly were.

He'd traveled the world, both in the military and

for pleasure, and had seen stunning women all over the globe. But Viv, who managed to embody innocence, class and a touch of sultriness, was one woman he couldn't get out of his mind.

Jack knew Viv would be gorgeous in anything she wore. That Native American heritage of hers set her apart from nearly every woman he knew. And the fact that she stood out in his mind only added to his guilt. He had to get a grip or he'd mess up their working relationship, and he refused to find another assistant. Viv was invaluable and they worked smoothly as a team.

And she was the only one he trusted to get inside the O'Sheas' inner sanctum and bring back information.

"Sorry I'm late." She blew out a breath, hugged little Katie closer to her chest. "She's been a little fussy and I'm pretty sure her teeth are bothering her."

Jack shoved his hands in his pockets. He had no experience with teething babies...not that he wouldn't have welcomed it once. But that chance was stolen from him the night his pregnant wife had been in the wrong place at the wrong time.

Working with Viv seriously hit his emotions from every single angle. Self-control was key to him not losing his ever-loving mind. And if he focused on the task at hand, at bringing down the O'Sheas, then nothing else mattered.

"I hope I didn't hold you up." Viv glanced at the table, her eyes wide. "Wow. You really went all out."

The yeast rolls, the turkey roulade with plum

sauce, the roasted potatoes and veggies, wine…even pats of butter in the shape of doves. Tilly, his chef, housekeeper and wanna-be matchmaker, had gone a bit overboard. And Jack knew for a fact there was a homemade red velvet cheesecake waiting for them in the kitchen.

He gave a mental shrug. Tilly's attempts were all in vain. Regardless of the fact that Jack had told her this dinner was strictly business, she clearly had ignored him and done her own thing…as usual.

Tilly had been his chef for nearly a decade and never missed a chance to set him up with a woman. Jack had turned down numerous blind dates she'd foisted on him. When he was ready, he could find his own damn date. Considering he was married to Carson Enterprises and dedicated to working for justice, he didn't have time to worry about dating or keeping a woman happy.

Jack glanced at the overly romantic table, then back to Viv. "I told Tilly this was a business dinner, but she's hell-bent on marrying me off."

Viv quirked a dark brow. "Well, this is already better than nearly every date I've been on. I'm still recovering from the last one."

Before Jack could ask what she meant, not that it was his business, Katie let out a cry. Viv patted her back and rocked back and forth, whispering comforting words in an attempt to calm the baby. Nothing seemed to be working, but he wasn't exactly an expert…nor would he ever be.

"I left the diaper bag up front where Tilly hung our coats. Could you grab it for me?"

Diaper bag. Sure. Maybe this meeting would have been better suited to a phone call. Viv had her hands full, technically working two jobs and caring for an eleven-month-old baby.

Jack refused to feel guilty as he headed to retrieve the diaper bag. Viv had been with him long enough and she was a strong woman. He wasn't worried she couldn't pull this off. He was *counting* on her to pull this off.

And that irritated him on a certain level. He hated relying on someone else to get the job done. He was a hands-on guy, so waiting for her to feed him information was not his idea of a dream job. But the FBI was counting on him to uncover something that would tie the O'Sheas to the crimes against the Parkers. Then they would have the open door to search the rest of their dealings.

The gray-and-white-patterned bag sat next to the accent table by the front door. Jack grabbed the strap and jerked the heavy bag up onto his shoulder. What the hell was in this thing? How could someone so small need so much stuff?

He started back down the hallway, but stopped short when Tilly stepped through the wide arched opening leading into the kitchen.

"Everything all right, Mr. Carson?"

Mr. Carson. She'd worked for him for nearly ten years and he'd given up trying to get her to call him by his first name. Tilly epitomized respect. Ironic, considering she didn't mind nosing right on into his love life…or lack thereof.

"Fine, Tilly. Thank you. Viv just needed her diaper bag."

Tilly smiled, the corners of her eyes creasing. "That little girl is lucky to have Ms. Smith in her life."

Jack nodded. "You're off duty from playing cupid tonight." And every other night.

A smile spread across her face, deepening the fan of wrinkles around her eyes. "I don't know what you're talking about," she claimed as she turned back to the kitchen. She stopped, threw a glance over her shoulder and added, "Just let me know when to serve the cheesecake for two."

"I'll serve it," he told her with a laugh. How could he not admire her determination, even if it was wasted? "Why don't you go on home?"

Her eyes all but sparkled. "Want to be alone? I get it. Consider me gone."

He wasn't going to correct her. Yes, he wanted to be alone with Viv, but not for the reasons Tilly assumed. She'd draw her own conclusions no matter what Jack said, so he wasn't wasting his breath. Besides, he never let Tilly in on his cases. Keeping his work to himself was the only way he managed to crack cases and find justice for the people he helped. The money was just a bonus.

Tilly argued that he was too busy traveling for work and making money to find a woman. She often hinted that all that money was a waste if he had no-body to spend it on.

As much as the thought of another woman in his life terrified him, Jack couldn't fault Tilly for her efforts. The woman's heart was in the right place—he just wished she'd give up. He'd had the love of his life once. That kind of love didn't happen twice.

As far as dating, well, he didn't want to worry about that, either. He was perfectly content with the way things were. Worrying about himself was enough.

But part of him, okay a huge part, worried about Viv when she was with the O'Sheas. He'd be a fool not to worry. So much for not getting personally in-volved.

Katie's cry pulled him away from his thoughts as he headed back onto the patio. Viv sat in one of the cushioned chairs at the table. She was muttering nur-turing words and holding Katie in a cradle position.

Jack froze when he spotted the pale pink lace peeking from beneath Viv's suit jacket. *Mercy, not again.* Katie had a white-knuckled grip on the V and was pulling the material apart.

The lace was quite the contrast against Viv's dark skin…skin he shouldn't be looking at and lace his fingers shouldn't be itching to trace.

*Pull it together.*

He adjusted the diaper bag on his shoulder and attempted to ignore the fact this woman loved lace lingerie.

"What do you need out of here?" he asked, un-zipping the bag.

She lifted her head and every time those dark eyes clashed with his, he struggled to look away. She had a power she wasn't even aware of and he'd do good to remind himself she was off-limits.

"Just set it down. I can get it."

Setting the bag at her feet, he stepped back and took a seat across from her. Unfortunately, when she bent down to dig inside the bag, Katie's grip tight-ened and that V only widened. A little pink bow was nestled in the middle of her breasts.

Damn it all. How the hell could he conduct a "business" meeting like this?

"Just tell me what you're looking for."

He got to his feet and picked the bag up, forcing himself not to look her way. *Focus on the bag.* That was the only way they were going to get anywhere this evening.

"Oh, the pain reliever." Viv shifted Katie on her lap, then adjusted her controversial jacket. "It's a small pink-and-white bottle with a dropper lid."

What the hell was a dropper lid? He shuffled through diapers, wipes, jars of baby food, lotion, a stuffed doll...

"Sorry. The outside pouch. I put it in there so it would be easily accessible."

Of course she had.

Jack finally pulled out the right thing and handed it to her. With his hands on his hips, he stood back and watched as Katie settled back against Viv's arm.

"It's okay, sweetheart." Viv put the medicine in her mouth, then seemed to be rubbing it on Katie's gums. "You'll feel better in just a minute."

Viv had brought Katie into his office a couple times when her neighbor wasn't available to baby-sit. During those occasions, Jack found a reason to step out for the day. Being near this combination of beautiful woman and enchanting baby was like getting smacked in the face with all he'd lost…his family being the sole reason he was determined to bring down those who kept skirting the law.

As Jack watched Viv console a fussy Katie, he couldn't help but wonder what his life would've been like had his wife lived. He tried not to go there in his mind, but sometimes that just wasn't possible.

"Sorry." Viv looked up at him with a soft smile. "Why don't you go ahead and eat. I'd hate to hold you up any longer."

Thankful for the chance to focus on something else, Jack started filling both of their plates. "How was today? Did you work with Laney?"

Laney O'Shea, the baby of the clan, was now engaged to Ryker Barrett, right-hand man and family enforcer. The two were expecting their first child in the summer and Jack hated the jealousy that rolled through him. People like that shouldn't get to experience the happiness that had been robbed from him.

"What?" she looked up at him, then back to the baby. "Oh, yeah. Laney was there all day."

"Any interesting clients?" he asked. "Did Ryker or her brothers stop in?"

Viv eased the baby up onto her shoulder, patting her back in an attempt to calm her. "Ryker dropped by and brought Laney lunch. He's been pretty territorial and protective of her since she got pregnant."

Gritting his teeth, Jack set her full plate in front of her. "Did he do anything else? Use the computers, make a call?"

"No. He was actually in and out in about ten minutes." Viv looked down to her plate. "There's no way I'll eat all of this."

"Eat what you want. Tilly takes any leftovers to the homeless shelter by her house. She actually always makes extra and takes it there anyway."

Viv stilled, her hand resting on Katie's back. "That's so sweet."

Jack shrugged. "She's got a big heart and she doesn't mind using my money to help others."

Katie's cries had calmed. Either the meds had kicked in or the poor thing was exhausted from crying.

Viv picked up her fork and stabbed one roasted potato. "And what about you? I'd say your heart is big or you wouldn't let her use your money for such things."

"I have no problem helping anyone when I see the need." He stared across the table, realizing she hadn't looked at him since mentioning work and was now trying to steer the conversation into another territory. "I grew up with a single mother who worked hard to make sure we never wanted for anything. I figure she struggled raising me alone. I would often hear her crying at night when she thought I was asleep."

Jack stopped, not wanting to dig too far into his suppressed memories. The past could easily cripple him, pull him down. The only thing he could use his past for was to propel him forward, to always remember where he came from. And he'd never forget the mother who sacrificed so much.

He pulled in a breath, determined to get back on track. "What happened today at the office?"

Her fork clattered to the plate, but she quickly picked it back up and shrugged. "Nothing. Just the same daily routine."

Again, the lack of eye contact. He'd known Viv long enough, hell, he'd been a soldier and investigator long enough, to know when someone was lying. What was going on?

Slowly, without taking his eyes off her, he leaned forward in his seat. "What happened today?" he repeated, slower this time until she finally looked directly at him.

"Jack, I'm telling you what happened." Now she held his eyes. Katie had fallen asleep and lay across Viv's arm, curled into Viv's body. "We were busy this morning with a new client and Laney handled that. I stayed in the back and logged inventory for the spring auction."

He listened, easing back in his cushioned seat. Why was he doubting her? He'd never second-guessed her before and she was his most trusted ally in this quest. He wouldn't have put her in this position if he didn't trust her completely.

"And then Ryker came with lunch," she went on. Her eyes darted down to the sleeping baby. "After that it was slow for about an hour and Laney and I ended up in the office talking baby things. She knows I foster and she had some questions."

"Like what?" He literally wanted every detail of what went on in that office. The key to his case was in there and he was not going to rest until every possible avenue was explored.

Viv shrugged. "She was asking about different milestones at different ages. But I've never had an infant until now. My foster children have always been older. The youngest I'd had was three."

Jack knew why Viv's taking Katie in deviated from her normal pattern of only fostering older children. One, she'd worked with the Parkers when they'd come into O'Shea's so she had a mild connection. According to Viv, she'd even played with little Katie during one of their visits.

Two, she knew the system was overloaded. Because she was certified to take in children, and since she was more than aware of the tragic situation, she'd actually asked to foster Katie.

"About an hour before we closed, an elderly lady came in and wanted to discuss some pieces she wanted to sell. She claimed they were from her honeymoon in Rome and thought they were valuable art."

Intrigued, Jack tipped his head. "What were they?"

Viv picked up her fork and took a bite of her potato. "I'm not sure. She had some pictures, but didn't want to bring the actual pieces without talking to Laney first."

That all sounded like a typical, boring day. A day that didn't help him one bit. But something was off. Viv had literally frozen when he'd first mentioned her workday at O'Shea's, then she wouldn't look at him.

"You're sure that's all?" he asked.

She shifted Katie to the other arm, which only aided in pulling her jacket open a bit more when Katie's hand got caught in the V. Viv did readjust the gap, but not before he was awarded another view of the swell of her breast.

"I'm just stressed," she assured him with a smile. "Katie is teething and the auction is going to be here before we know it. Working at O'Shea's isn't just me snooping and eavesdropping. They expect me to actually do a job, so it's tiresome at times."

Not to mention all the work she was doing for him. She was technically a single mother working two part-time jobs. But that part-time added up and when he was constantly meeting her outside of business hours, that didn't help. Damn it, he was ready to wrap this case up and let the justice system take care of this mob family. But he had to be patient. It was a trait he hated, yet it was necessary in his line of work.

With Katie resting peacefully, Viv continued to eat. Jack didn't press the topic again. He didn't know if he was just reading too much into her actions or if she was truly just stressed, but he wasn't about to add more to her plate.

"They don't suspect you, right?"

Viv took a sip of her wine. "They suspect everyone who's been in and out of that office. But, not me specifically. I'm careful, Jack."

Why was his name on her lips like a tight ball of lust hitting his gut? He couldn't afford the distraction—especially when it came to his damn assistant.

When this case was over, he'd head to his villa in Italy. He could relax, find a woman to spend a meaningless night with. He clearly was not thinking straight and he blamed everything on being overworked and sexually frustrated.

"There is a new shipment of paintings coming in on Monday," Viv went on, oblivious to the turn in his thoughts. "I'm supposed to be off, but I thought I'd see if I could come in and just tell them I'd like some extra hours."

Jack curled his fingers around the tumbler of bourbon and considered her idea. "I wouldn't. They already know someone is leaking information. If you ask for extra time, that could be a red flag. I need you to do everything as you always had before."

Viv nodded. "I guess that makes sense. I just wish there was more I could do."

Taking a hearty, warm gulp of his favorite twenty-year bourbon, Jack wished there was more to be done. But he wasn't inside, and using Viv as his eyes and ears was the only thing he could do at this point.

"I'd rather you explore the Parkers' angle," he

told her, easing back in his seat and glancing at the sleeping baby. "You have the perfect lead-in, especially when you're with Laney. Continue to talk about Katie, discuss how she's adjusting, throw in the loss of her parents and you've opened up the floor."

Viv pushed her plate back, wrapped both arms around the baby and pursed her lips. "That could work. Laney and I tend to always discuss the baby when we're not talking about the auction."

"Now's the time. That's the angle we need to work. If we can find out more about the night they were killed, I know it will circle us right back to the O'Sheas."

Jack didn't care what the initial charges were. This corrupt family had plenty of crimes they could be pinned with. But first he needed concrete evidence that proved the O'Sheas weren't so squeaky clean.

No matter who was in charge now that Patriarch Patrick O'Shea had passed, this family was into illegals so deep, there was no way they could've gotten out in such a short time.

"I'll be there from eight to noon tomorrow," she reminded him, as if he didn't have her schedule memorized down to the very last second. "I need to take Katie to the doctor for a checkup, so I'll text you when I leave work."

When Katie started to stir, Viv came to her feet. Rocking gently back and forth, Viv patted the baby's back in an attempt to calm her once again. Jack watched as she instantly went into mother mode. Viv was the most giving person he'd ever known. A born nurturer. He'd checked her background thoroughly before hiring her, so he knew she'd never married or had kids. He'd seen quite a bit of hospitalizations when she'd been young, but she'd never mentioned an illness, so he never asked. He could've easily found out, but he'd snooped enough and didn't want to betray her trust at this point. Honesty was of the utmost importance to him and he expected it to be a two-way street.

"I should get her home," Viv stated. "She needs to rest and I need to get my own downtime or I'll be of no use to anyone."

Viv wasn't a superhero, though she was a working foster mother juggling two jobs and carrying a colossal lie on her shoulders, so that was pretty much the same thing. Jack set his napkin on the table and rose to stand in front of her.

"Why don't you see if your neighbor can watch Katie for a few hours extra each day so you can relax?" he suggested. "I'll pay for it if that's an issue."

Viv's brows shot up. "I don't care about the money, Jack. The reason I became a foster mother was to care for children who don't have anyone. Pawning Katie off on my neighbor just so I can nap will never be an option."

"That's not what I meant," he retorted, though she'd made him look uncaring, which was not the case. He cared...too much. "If you don't look out for yourself, how do you expect to do everything else?"

Her lids lowered, her breath came out on a deep sigh. She shook her head before meeting his gaze.

"Everything I do is for those I care about. This child, you. I have no family, Jack, so I work to fill a void. When I stop working, when I stop caring for those around me, I start to think. I don't want the down time. I can't mentally afford it. Do you get what I'm saying?"

Jack swallowed the lump in his throat. How could she put his thoughts, his emotions, into such perfect terms? It was like they lived a parallel life, and he desperately wanted to know what made her this way. Why did she use work as her coping mechanism?

He'd already known she had no family. He of all people understood the need to connect with something in life and he clung to work...apparently so did she. He'd never heard her so passionate about it before, but he understood the ache, the emptiness that needed to be filled.

"You're talking to the workaholic," he told her, trying to lighten the intensity of the mood. "I just wanted to make sure you were taken care of, as well."

Shoulders squared, she tipped her head. "I assure you, I'm fine. But I do need to get home and I promise I'll text you tomorrow. We'll get this," she assured him. "We've come this far, we'll make it the rest of the way."

Jack helped her with the diaper bag, then assisted her with her coat and Katie's coat—which was no easy feat, considering she was still asleep.

Once Viv was gone, Jack leaned against the front door and stared into the empty two-story foyer. Yeah, he understood perfectly about not having anyone.

He'd bought this massive home in Beacon Hill after his wife died. He couldn't stay in the small cottage he'd bought for her, the place where they'd planned to start their family. While he'd wanted to burn the cottage to the ground, he ended up selling it to a young newlywed couple who had the same dreams he'd once had.

He'd moved on, made more money than he knew what to do with and when he started looking for a permanent residence, he knew he wanted something large…something he'd never be able to fill with a family. He wanted the space so it didn't feel like the walls were closing in on him.

Some might say he was flashing, living in a huge house all by himself, but he didn't care. His cars, his vacation home in the mountains, the two homes overseas, they were all material things he'd give up in a second to have someone in his life.

No. Not someone. His wife.

Yet lately, when he would think of someone to share his wealth with, Viv kept popping up. He wanted to scrub that image from his mind because thinking of another woman was surely a betrayal to Carly…right?

As he headed down the hall and passed the kitchen, he instantly remembered the cheesecake. If Tilly came back in the morning and saw that none of it had been eaten, she'd be disappointed.

Easy fix. He'd be gone before she came in and he'd take it to the office with him.

Or he could take it somewhere else.

Viv claimed she didn't need anyone to look after her, but that was a lie. And Jack would take on the role in the name of business…because that's all he had time for in his life.

Whatever notions he had in his head about Viv, he had to remember she was his assistant. She could never be anything else.

# Three

With Katie turning one next week, Viv had decided that the baby's shots were going to have to happen on her half day at O'Shea's.

Now that the doctor's visit was—mercifully—over, Viv was convinced the shots had hurt her more than they'd hurt Katie. Viv had just walked into her apartment, dumped the diaper bag next to the sofa and put Katie in her Pack 'n Play when someone knocked on her door.

She couldn't suppress the groan that escaped her. She was soaked to the bone from the chilly rain. All she wanted to do was strip off her wet suit and get into her cozy pajamas. Viv had been able to shield Katie from the elements by wrapping her inside her coat and holding Katie's favorite blanket over the tot's head. Now Viv needed to get that blanket into the dryer or there would be hell to pay come bedtime.

The pounding on the door persisted. What were the odds she could ignore her unwanted guest? If she lived in a house, maybe, but in an apartment building she couldn't have her neighbors put out.

"Vivianna?" Jack's voice boomed and Viv realized her wish to pretend no one was out there had just vanished.

She crossed the floor, her shoes squishing. She wasn't even going to glance at her reflection in the mirror next to the door. The drowned-rat look wasn't becoming on anyone.

Flicking the lock, Viv opened the door. Of course Jack didn't have one drop of rain on him. The large black umbrella he held at his side was dripping.

"You're..."

"Soaked," she finished. "I know. Come on in."

She stood back so he didn't have to brush against her as he stepped inside. Katie made noises and clapped when she spotted Jack. Inwardly, Viv tended to have that same reaction, but she wasn't too keen on the fact that he was seeing her look so haggard and frumpy.

She'd really been confident this morning when she'd left for work in her gray pencil skirt and fitted, pale yellow sweater. She'd even taken extra time with her hair, since Katie had slept in. Now Viv must look like all she'd done this morning was shower... with her clothes on.

She was so over this winter weather. One day

it snowed, the next it rained. Spring couldn't come soon enough. But it was only February, meaning Valentine's Day was fast approaching. A holiday she could totally live without.

"I brought this for you."

Katie eyed the dish in his hand. She'd been too preoccupied with her looks to realize he held food.

Glorious food. She didn't even care if that domed plate held a bologna sandwich, her stomach growled at the sight. She'd skipped lunch because she'd left work late and had barely made it to Katie's appointment.

"Whatever it is, thank you," she said, taking the covered plate. She headed toward the kitchen, cringing as her shoes made the most unpleasant noises.

Of all the times Jack could see her, of all the times he *had* seen her, this was not her best moment. She set the dish on the counter and pulled the lid off. A laugh escaped her.

"Cheesecake?" she asked, turning to glance over her shoulder.

Jacked shrugged out of his suit jacket and hung it on the hook by the door…as if he'd done so a thousand times. Seeing a man's jacket hanging next to hers did funny things to her belly. Her eyes locked on the two pieces beside each other, and she didn't want to dwell on it too long, but couldn't get over the fact that this simple gesture seemed so intimate.

But he wasn't staying, he was visiting, for pity's sake. For a second, though, she wanted to pretend. He looked good in his all-black suit, with that rich, dark hair. He'd brought her cheesecake when she looked like a mess, and he didn't seem appalled by her appearance. If he wasn't the world's most perfect man, then one didn't exist.

Would he ever see her as more than an ally? As more than his assistant?

She hadn't missed the way he'd sneaked a peek at her cleavage last night. He was a guy; they all did it. But when she'd caught his gaze on her, everything inside her had warmed, tingled. Because he hadn't just looked and glanced away. No, there had been a hunger in his eyes she hadn't seen before.

"What are you doing here so early in the day?" she asked, turning to lean back against the counter. "Not that four o'clock is early, but you tend to work much later than this."

"I had a meeting today not far from here, so I thought I'd come by to see what happened at O'Shea's today."

Katie clanged her blocks together and squealed as she flung them out of her Pack 'n Play. Viv ignored them. This toss and fetch was an endless game and one she wasn't going to get sucked into.

"I need to get out of these wet clothes," she stated. "Can we talk after?"

His eyes raked over her wet body. Jack never needed words to get his point across. This powerful man had such a hold on her emotions, and he had no idea.

All this was her problem, she knew, but did he ever think of her outside of work? Not that she'd ever know. Jack's personal life was never on the table for discussion. She knew of Tilly, his right-hand woman, but that was all. Anyone else in Jack's life was there only because of work. To Viv's knowledge, he didn't even date...or if he did, he was extremely discreet.

"I'll wait in here," he finally told her.

Viv tiptoed through her kitchen and out into the hallway toward her bedroom. Once inside, she shut the door, thankful for the few moments to herself. She hadn't expected him to just show up, with carbs and calories no less, so she was even more taken aback than usual.

Before the O'Shea case, Jack had never showed up at her apartment. He'd texted and called after hours, but all pertaining to work. Granted, his recent home visits also centered around work, but he'd seriously stepped up his game in an attempt to bring the notorious family down.

Viv closed her eyes and pulled in a shaky breath. The fact that Patrick O'Shea's journal was hidden in her closet weighed heavily on her mind. Guilt, anxiety, fear...they all consumed her, making her question her next move.

She hadn't been lying when she said she had no one in her life. Keeping a relationship with Jack, no matter how platonic, was imperative.

She needed to tell him what she'd learned, but how did she do that without hurting him? The FBI trusted Jack, was counting on him, and he was counting on her. He sought justice like he needed it to live, so telling him about her discovery would cloud his judgment…and hurt him in a way that would alter their relationship.

She didn't want to hurt him, and finding out Patrick O'Shea was his father would most certainly destroy Jack. Still, he deserved to know. The question was, when should she tell him?

Viv made quick work of ridding herself of her wet clothes and shoes. She wasn't telling him today. She couldn't. There would be a right time, just…not now. Hopefully, a break in the case would come soon. Then she could give the journal to him and let him decide what to do with the information.

She didn't bother drying her hair, just twisted it up into a messy bun. After throwing on a pair of yoga pants and an off-the-shoulder sweatshirt, she headed back out into the living room.

Jack still remained closer to the kitchen than the living room. His gaze was directed across the open space at Katie, who was oblivious as she chewed on the fingers of her plush doll.

"Let's cut into that cheesecake and talk," Viv suggested. She needed something to occupy her hands, her mind, other than the journal in the other room and the unnerving effect Jack's presence had on her. "How did your meeting go?"

He didn't answer her. He never even looked her way.

"Do you think she knows the significant people in her life are gone?" he murmured, almost as if his thoughts had traveled out into the open without his knowledge. "I mean, she seems happy with you, but is she aware of the void?"

Viv thought of that often since Katie had come to live with her. The older kids she had fostered obviously knew all too well the reality of why they were in foster care. But sweet little Katie would have no idea why her world was suddenly so different.

"She says 'Mama' over and over, but I'm not sure if she's just babbling or actually asking for her. But I'm certain she notices the absence." Viv crossed her arms, stood beside Jack and watched his face. "Are you okay?"

He blinked as if waking from a trance. "It's been a long couple months. That's all."

When he turned to her, Viv stepped back. That intense gaze landed directly on hers and she had no idea what to do with the emotions stirring within her, from the guilt and anxiety over when and how to tell him about the journal, to the tension and chemistry that couldn't be ignored. It seemed unlikely she was the only one who felt the air crackling between them, yet Jack was in total control and never let on that he thought of her in any other way than simply his assistant.

But he'd shown up on her doorstep with red velvet cheesecake his chef had made.

"Tell me about your meeting."

He shook his head. "Later. I want to know what happened with you today."

"Not much," she admitted, then held up a hand to stop him when he opened his mouth. "But I overheard Laney and Braden talking. They said the FBI hadn't contacted them in a few days, but they were keeping their guard up. Braden told Laney not to erase any records and that he had nothing to hide in regards to the Parkers."

Jack's eyes held hers, but he said nothing. She wasn't delivering case-breaking news, but she had to tell him everything she'd heard, learned…except for the the piece of evidence that was burning a hole in her conscience.

"Something else happen?" he asked.

Viv pulled herself from her thoughts. Those midnight eyes still penetrated her, as if he were trying to read her thoughts…as if he *could* read her thoughts.

"Not today, but Braden said Mac was flying in on Monday and he'd be in the office all next week."

"Why?"

Viv shrugged. "They didn't say, but I'm working three full days next week and I'll find out then."

Jack raked a hand down his face and blew out a breath. "This is so damn frustrating. For years they flaunted their lifestyle in the face of law enforcement. Luckily, I work for myself and I don't have to stick so close to the rules."

Viv didn't want to see him struggle, didn't like that she'd found so little for him to go on. "I tried to engage Laney in conversation about the babies, but a client called and she was pulled away. Then I had to leave for Katie's doctor's appointment."

Jack shoved his hands in his pockets and glanced at the ceiling. Watching him battle with this frustration was more difficult than Viv had thought it would be. But she had to keep the journal to herself for now. Everything—absolutely everything, from his life to this case—would change in the matter of seconds as soon as he learned about it.

"You're in my office tomorrow." He regrouped and focused his attention back on her. "I want both of us to go over every bit of intel we have on this family. Maybe there's some tiny nugget of information we're missing. Something that can put us on the right track. I want you ready for next week, when everyone is here."

He was getting desperate, yet she understood his need to protect his reputation as being the best. Unfortunately, the journal she'd discovered wasn't the master key to solving this equation, and she had nothing else.

"Tell the Feds that all the players will be available next week," she went on, hoping to give him something useful, to buy them a bit more time. "With everyone at the office, something must be going on, or else they're worried about this investigation."

Jack leaned a shoulder against the wall and pinned her with his stare. "Maybe they have an idea who's been leaking the information."

The thought sent a shiver up her spine. Taking this job had been risky, but she'd agreed to let Jack create a solid cover for her. She'd put her life in his hands...literally, if all those rumors surrounding the O'Sheas were true. But Viv hadn't been afraid. Jack wouldn't let anything happen to her.

"I'm not getting that vibe," she replied as she moved into the kitchen. "Do you want a piece of this cheesecake or not, because if I eat the entire thing, I won't fit into my pencil skirts."

His eyes traveled the length of her body. How in the world did that man evoke more emotions and glorious sensations with one look than some men did with foreplay? Seriously. How did Jack make her want him so much, so deeply, when he wasn't even trying?

"Your figure is just fine, with or without the cheesecake."

Viv turned away, because that sultry tone of his sent a combination of shivers and thrills darting through her. Add in the way he'd assessed her body—such as it was, clad in yoga pants and a sweatshirt—and she wondered if maybe she'd pegged him wrong for not showing any interest and keeping his emotions all closed off.

Katie let out a squeal, breaking the tension. She seemed quite content to sit and play with her toys for a bit. Thankfully, her pain reliever had kicked in fast after the shots.

Once Viv had generous pieces of the decadent dessert on a couple saucers, she crossed to her two-seater table in the breakfast nook. Well, technically it was her breakfast nook, dining room and home office, depending on the time of day. Her apartment wasn't big, but it suited her needs. She rarely had guests unless it was foster children, so she didn't require a grand table. Besides, the place was close to Jack's office and the rent was perfect.

Though right now she did feel a little inadequate, remembering how amazing Jack's patio had been. He most likely had an exquisite dining room and an eat-in kitchen, yet he'd still set up dinner on his screened-in sunroom. Just the little bit she'd seen of his house had left her in awe. The rich wood, the clean lines of the furniture, that grand entryway with a masculine yet impressive chandelier suspended from the second floor were worthy of a magazine. Her entire apartment could fit into that foyer alone.

Jack either had a perfect eye for detail and decor or he'd hired someone to tastefully, expensively decorate his mansion. He took a seat across from her, but her round table proved to be smaller than she'd thought when his knees bumped hers. Why did his every single action get her body all tingly and jittery? This was Jack. Her boss. Her very sexy, very single, very mysterious boss. Other than the fact that he was a widower, never dated and had served in the military, she didn't know much else about his personal life…but oh, how she wanted to.

He scooped up a bite. "Tilly will be thrilled we're getting to this."

"Trust me, I'm more thrilled." Viv wasn't going to even think about calories right now. Turning down red velvet cheesecake would be a sin. "She's going to be happier to know you came to my apartment."

His eyes caught hers. "For business."

Right. Business. What else would he want from her?

"Still, she seems ready to make sure you have a woman in your life."

When he remained silent, Viv kept going. She would crack his shell at some point. Over the past couple years she'd worked for him, he'd not volunteered any information unless it pertained to a case. And the only reason Viv knew about his mother was that he always referred to her in the past tense. His father was never mentioned.

And Viv would've assumed Jack was a regular single guy had Tilly not slipped and said something about his "late wife." That had been at the office. One sharp look from Jack and the woman's lips were still sealed to this day.

"I don't know how your dating life has been—"

"Nonexistent."

Viv swallowed. She'd assumed as much...but why? He was, well, hot. He had money, not that a bank account made a man, but it wasn't like he couldn't get a woman. Maybe he just didn't want to. Maybe he had some other reason for being married to his work and ignoring the world around him.

"I really should consider going that route, because I've had some doozies."

*Doozies? Way to sound classy, Viv.*

Jack took another bite, obviously not feeling so chatty about his own personal life. Whatever. She was chatty enough for both of them, especially when she was a bit nervous. And between the attraction and the journal only a couple rooms away, she had plenty of unease spiraling through her.

"One time, I had a guy who offered me dinner and a movie."

"Predictable," Jack muttered.

"I can handle predictable," she added with a laugh. "It was the expectations he had for the evening. Cooking me a frozen pizza and binge-watching old movies wasn't my idea of a night out. He was shocked when I made an excuse to leave. He seriously thought…"

Jack laid his fork down and narrowed his eyes. "You're kidding? Tell me you didn't."

Viv tipped her head. "I do have standards, Jack. It takes more than a frozen pizza to get me into bed."

Those bright eyes held hers, then dipped to her mouth before traveling back up. "What does it take?"

# Four

$W$here the hell had that question come from?

This was why Jack had always refused to get personally involved with anyone. Yet here he was, asking his *assistant* what it took to get her into bed.

Clearly the case, and working so closely with this breathtaking woman, was making him delirious.

"Well—"

"No." Jack held up his hand. "Don't answer that."

Viv quirked a brow, taunting him with a teasing smile. "You're sure?"

There could be no flirting, no unwanted attraction. Too much was at stake—the case, his sanity.

When he remained silent, she laughed. "We'll just say that it takes more than a lame dinner and a black-and-white movie."

Jack laughed with her. He couldn't help himself. "Any man who doesn't pull out all the stops for you is an idiot."

She tipped her head again, pursing her lips. "You never do that."

Easing back in his seat, Jack met Viv's eyes across the small table. "Laugh? No, I don't."

She crossed her arms and rested her elbows on the table. "Why not? What do you do for fun?"

"Stakeouts."

She rolled her eyes just as Katie let out a cry. "I'm serious," she stated as she rose to her feet.

Jack watched as she maneuvered through the living room to Katie. The little girl instantly extended her arms to reach for Viv. Jack turned away. All this…familial life was digging into that past wound, threatening to tear it wide open.

Some might say he was hard, uncaring, detached. Whatever it took to stay sane, to stay on top of his game, to help bring criminals down—to find justice… Jack didn't care what label he was given.

He concentrated on taking the empty plates to the kitchen and placing them in the sink. Resting his hands on the edge of the counter, he pulled in a breath. He shouldn't have come by. Venturing into Viv's world, into her damn apartment, was not smart.

In his defense, he'd been close and she hadn't texted, and he wanted to bring the dessert, so he'd broken his own rule of not getting into someone else's personal space. Time to head back home, where he could hide in his office, drink his bourbon and contemplate his next move. He was done waiting around for the O'Sheas to slip up.

When he turned, he found Viv standing close to him...too close. So near he could see the dark flecks in her eyes.

"Something wrong?" she asked, her brows drawn in.

Katie pulled on Viv's still-damp hair. All that gorgeous, silky, midnight-black hair. He'd be lying to himself if he pretended he hadn't envisioned that mass spread out over his navy sheets. When had this woman gone from assistant to starring in his fantasies? Lately, the line between professional and personal was becoming more and more blurry.

Even from the start, when he'd interviewed her, he hadn't denied her beauty. But after a few years of working together closely, and especially this past year, the dreams were becoming more frequent. Forget the fact that he vowed never to open himself up again; he was a professional having extremely unprofessional thoughts.

"I'll let you get on with your evening," he told her, ignoring the worried look on her face. She need not be concerned about him. His emotions had been murdered along with his wife, years ago. "I'll be sure to tell Tilly you enjoyed her dessert."

Viv seemed as if she wanted to say something else, but finally nodded and stepped aside to let him through. "If she wants to bake anything else and send it my way, she's more than welcome. I have a sweet tooth."

"I'm aware." Jack nodded toward the bowl of chocolate candy on the counter. "Your desk at work has a matching bowl."

Viv shrugged as Katie continued to pull on her hair. "I won't apologize for my snacks."

If those snacks were what kept that body all curvy and mesmerizing in skirts, then he'd buy her a full year's supply.

No, damn it, he wouldn't. Admiring her body wasn't his job as her boss. He had to get the hell out of here before he made an absolute fool of himself. Sitting at her little table, watching her with Katie… it was all too much. She smelled too damn good and had that rumpled, sexy look down pat. The rain she'd been caught in hadn't done a thing to diminish her beauty.

If circumstances were different—if he wasn't a jaded widower, her boss and her protector on this job —then maybe he'd seduce her. Maybe then he'd exorcise her right out of his system.

"Why are you looking at me like that?" she asked.

He still hadn't moved, even though she'd made an opening for him to pass. Jack stepped forward, his eyes on hers.

"I've never seen you out of your professional element. I just…"

"What?"

Hell, he didn't know. Wanted to touch her? Kiss her? To know if either of those would compare to his detailed thoughts of having her in his bed?

Viv shifted Katie in her arms, reached out and

placed her hand on his shoulder. Jack stilled. Such a simple touch shouldn't evoke instant bedroom fantasies.

"Everything will work out with this case," she assured him. "We're getting closer. I just know it."

Yes. Let her think his moment of becoming a mute, staring fool had to do with stress from the case. The last thing he needed was for her to believe he was attracted to her. Hell, if she thought that, who knew what would happen?

Wait. He knew exactly what would happen… which was why he had to get out of here before he turned his thoughts into actions.

"I'll see you in the morning."

With that, he got the hell out. Maybe the chilly rain would cool him off and draw his thoughts back to the job—and not his assistant splayed across his bed.

The rain had stopped, but had quickly turned to snow. As if in tune with the crappy, depressing weather, Viv's morning had gone downhill fast.

First her blow-dryer had gone kaput after about one minute of drying her hair. Then Katie had a blowout in her diaper, so that called for a change of every single item of clothing, from her onesie to her shoes. How did babies have that much in them that they could ruin an entire outfit?

To top everything off, Martha was sick and unable to babysit. Lovely. But nothing Viv couldn't manage. She had thrown her wet hair in a side braid and changed Katie into something fresh. Unfortunately, there was no backup sitter. So here she was, wrestling the diaper bag, a sack of toys and Katie into the office. At least she was with Jack today and not at O'Shea's.

After Jack left her apartment last night, she couldn't help but reflect on their conversation…or the way he'd looked at her. The dynamics had silently shifted between them. She wasn't sure what had changed, what he'd been thinking or why he'd been staring at her like he wanted…well, her.

The shiver racing through her body had nothing to do with the February arctic breeze and everything to do with the possibilities swirling through her mind.

Maybe it was the fact that Valentine's Day was next week. Perhaps all the hearts and cupids in the storefronts were messing with her mind. When was the last time she'd actually had a valentine?

If Jack was having thoughts of her, would he ever act on them? Would he make a move, or was he that removed from the emotional world that he'd keep everything professional between them?

What if she weren't his assistant? Would that change the game?

So many questions. Thankfully, Viv had Katie to think about, and her first birthday was next week, which could cancel out any Valentine's Day celebration. Not that Viv had dates lined up, but now she had an excuse to ignore the day not created for single women.

Warmth enveloped her as she stepped inside the office. The inviting brownstone had once been Jack's apartment, before he turned it into a permanent office. The place was cozy, yet professional, with neutral colors and leather sofas. It felt more like a home than a workplace. Viv didn't mind bringing Katie here because she could easily section her off from the front area, where clients might be.

Once the door closed behind them, she breathed a sigh of relief and dropped her bags to the floor. If nothing else, by the end of her time with Katie, Viv would have toned arms.

She didn't want to think about giving Katie up to her adoptive family. Letting go of any child was always a bittersweet moment, but Katie was special.

Viv had never met the parents of any of her other foster kids. But she'd met with the Parkers on more than one occasion. She and Katie shared a unique bond Viv couldn't deny, but she would have to continue to guard her heart or she'd be crushed in the end. Not being able to have children of her own was a bitter pill to swallow, so getting too attached to Katie would only cause her more heartache.

Jack came out of his office and glanced at the mess at Viv's feet. "What's wrong?"

Holding a bundled-up Katie, Viv merely shrugged. "It's been a crazy morning of trying to get ready and learning Martha wasn't able to watch Katie. That snow is coming down pretty fast and I have no sitter."

He wasted no time in crossing to her and bending to retrieve her bags. "You could've taken the day off."

"There's too much work to do," Viv stated, as she wrestled the hat and coat off Katie.

Gripping her bags, Jack headed toward the back, where her office was located. "We could've phoned or emailed," he called over his shoulder. "I'm not that much of a slave driver that I expect you to take her out in this mess."

This wasn't the first time she'd had to bring Katie, so Viv had invested in a small play yard for her office. This way the door could stay closed, and there was an entertaining area for Katie to explore while Viv worked. The brownstone had two spacious bedrooms that Jack had converted into offices. He also happened to keep a sofa in his office that converted to a bed…which she knew he often used instead of going home.

Viv sat Katie in the designated kid area in the corner and turned to take off her own coat. Jack had set the bags on the long accent table against the back wall and was closing the distance between them.

Why did her boss have to smell so good? And why did she have to be tortured by it?

"I expect you to tell me when you need a break."

Viv untied her wrap coat and draped it across the back of her desk chair. Smoothing her silk blouse down over her pencil skirt, she attempted to calm her nerves. She'd lain awake most of the night worried about that journal.

Correction. She'd read the journal the first half of the night, then had stared into the darkness the other half, terrified of Jack's reaction once he discovered the truth.

From the veiled hints penned in Patrick O'Shea's neat hand, Jack was indeed the patriarch's son. Jack's mother had wanted to keep their affair a secret. Though, according to the timeline, Patrick and Jack's mother had been an item shortly after Patrick lost his wife.

Most likely the man had turned to her only for comfort. But according to the journal, he'd been torn up over not having his son in his life. The reasons seemed valid enough. Jack's mother didn't want her child to be exposed to the O'Shea lifestyle, and she worried what would happen if Jack were given the infamous last name. The affair wasn't created out of love, but from Patrick's tone, Viv could tell he cared for her.

Regardless of Patrick's past feelings or intentions, Jack wouldn't care. He'd be furious learning who his family was. All this time he'd thought he had nobody, but the family he was hell-bent on bringing down shared the same blood.

Every time he mentioned his mother, Catherine Carson, his tone held pure affection and adoration. Jack was a loyal man, which was why the pain he'd endured too often had hardened him. He was protecting himself.

"Sit down."

Viv jerked back. "Excuse me?"

Jack reached around her, turning her chair until it bumped the backs of her knees. When he curled his hands around her shoulders, she stilled. Oh, those hands were powerful as they pushed her into the seat. His eyes never left hers as he loomed over her.

"If you exhaust yourself to the point you can't work, you're no good to me."

Viv shivered, from her damp hair, from his stare... from his low tone that resembled anger, though there was concern in those eyes staring back at her.

"I'm off tomorrow," she reminded him. "I can rest up then. But if I needed a day off, I would've told you."

His gaze flickered to Katie, then back. This wasn't the first time she'd noticed how uncomfortable he seemed around the little girl.

"Does this bother you? Her being here?"

Jack shook his head. "Of course not. I'm just not experienced with babies, that's all."

She knew he had no kids of his own, and he was an only child, so it made sense that he was nervous. But there was almost a level of sadness there—an emotion she recognized all too well.

"What's got you so nervous?" she asked.

Jack eased to his full height, crossed his arms over his chest and stared down at her. The intimidating stance might work on some, but Viv saw right through him. She wasn't a stranger to defense mechanisms herself.

"I need to answer a couple of emails, then we can start working," he stated, obviously changing the subject.

Viv slowly came to her feet, not at all surprised

when he didn't back up. "I never took you for someone who runs away from confrontation."

Jack's eyes swept over her, then up again to meet
her gaze. "I never run from anything."

"No?" she retorted. "You're married to your job,
you don't date and the sight of a child has you twitch-
ing. I'd say you're running from several things."

Viv ignored his sneer. Sometimes people just
needed to be called out on things. Perhaps not her
boss, but she couldn't stand her curiosity anymore.
She'd worked for him so long, yet he never, ever
opened up. How did anyone live so closed off for that
long? It was like he bounced between the office and
his mansion. What did he do at home in that empty,
sprawling house?

He traveled for work, always alone, but that was
all the man did. Living a robotic life with very little
meaningful interaction sounded so hollow, so depressing.

"Not everyone is so open with their personal lives,
Viv."

Why did her name sound so sexy coming through
those kissable lips?

"When was the last time *you* dated?" he added,
quirking a dark brow as if he'd bested her.

"The day before Katie came to live with me." There.
That should wipe that smirk off his face. "And you?"

The muscles in his jaw ticked. "Instead of digging
into my personal life, why don't we dig in to work?"

Viv shrugged. "Fine with me. I need to get Katie
settled and give her a snack. Go send your emails."

When she turned to ease her chair back, Jack's hand curled around her arm. Viv glanced from his strong fingers over her silk blouse up to his eyes.

"You may want to rethink giving me commands." That low, throaty tone washed over her, the warmth from his touch piercing right through to her heart. "And always remember who's in charge."

Oh, he could be "in charge" of her any time he wanted. But now would be a good time to keep her mouth shut. Apparently she'd hit her mark. If the hunger in his eyes was any indication, Jack wasn't thinking of her as just his assistant anymore.

Good. It was time he was as uncomfortable as she was, because she'd been keeping her sexual frustrations in check for too long.

He released her, but didn't step back. "Be ready in twenty minutes."

Viv nodded, letting him think he could throw his weight around. Fine. Whatever. This was his office, he was her boss, but they both knew she'd knocked him off his game earlier.

Jack took a step back and shoved his hands into his pockets. "Call the deli on the corner and have lunch delivered at noon. I want—"

"A Reuben with half the corned beef, no pickle on the side, no chips and a piece of carrot cake."

When he raised his brows and smiled, Viv added, "This isn't our first lunch stuck in the office."

Katie started screaming, "Up, up, up."

Viv laughed. "Sorry. Her new word apparently is *up*."

Brushing past Jack, Viv approached the Pack 'n Play. Those sweet little arms stretched toward her. Katie clearly needed the comfort that only human contact could provide. Viv understood that yearning.

After settling Katie onto her hip, Viv turned back to Jack, who remained exactly where she'd left him. "I'll be ready in a few minutes. She just needs some love right now."

The muscle in his jaw ticked again. "Does she do that often? Want you to hold her?"

Katie rested her head on Viv's shoulder. Viv knew of nothing sweeter than to be a comfort for a grieving child. Even if there was no possible way Katie understood the grief, she understood the void.

"She seems to be clingier than when she first came." Viv wrapped her arms around the little girl, holding her firmly against her chest. "It's almost like she realizes now that certain people aren't coming back into her life."

Viv was extremely careful never to say *mommy* or *daddy*. She didn't want to trigger any painful emotions in Katie. But at the same time, Viv hated acting as if the Parkers had never been part of the child's life. Hopefully, the family that adopted Katie would tell her about the amazing parents she'd had.

Jack eased around the desk, but didn't get too close to her as he kept his eyes on Katie. "I will bring them down," he vowed. "It won't bring her parents back, but there will be justice."

The conviction in his voice, the anger flaring in his eyes, brought on a fresh wave of guilt. How could she help him bring down his own family? Would he want to bring them down if he knew the truth?

Pulling herself together, Viv crossed the office to the table. As would anyone experienced with children, she used a one-hand grab to find snacks in the diaper bag.

"Just give me a few minutes," she told him. "Then I'll be ready."

She continued to shuffle items until Jack left the room. Once he was gone, Viv closed her eyes, resting her forehead against Katie's. Because at the root of all this chaos, the lies, the unknowns…the fear, there was an innocent child who deserved to be Viv's top priority. Every action, every decision right now revolved around Katie and her welfare. The journal, the secret—none of that mattered in the grand scheme of things. Viv would put Katie ahead of her own needs, her own wishes and even what was morally right, if need be.

Even if it cost everything with Jack once he realized she'd lied and withheld the ultimate secret.

# Five

Jack eased back in the leather club chair opposite Viv's desk as she reached for yet more pieces of candy from her little glass dish. He wondered if she even realized she was doing so. She scrolled through the items on her computer screen with one hand, and used the other for snacking.

He could watch her eat candy all day. His body tightened as her tongue darted out to catch a stray piece of chocolate on her bottom lip. Why was he so turned on by such a simple movement? He knew why—because it was Viv.

"The notes I have copies of are all clean," she stated softly. Katie finally had fallen asleep in her Pack 'n Play after lunch, so they had to talk quietly. "There's no red flags on shipments, nothing that looks suspicious in the days leading up to the Parkers' deaths. On the evening of the robbery, Ryker and Laney were out to dinner with Braden and Zara. Mac and Jenna were in Florida at the Miami location. They haven't deviated from their stories even once."

Jack eased forward, resting his elbows on his knees and raking his hands through his hair. "I'm going to call a meeting with Braden."

Viv jerked around in her seat. "What?"

He saw no other way. Jack had already put the pressure on Ryker, the family henchman. If that didn't work to Jack's satisfaction, he'd go straight to the top, and that meant the oldest of the O'Sheas.

"You can't do that," she went on. "They'll know who you are if you go to them."

"It's a chance I'm willing to take."

Viv leaned her forearms on her desk as her worried gaze held his. "You were at Braden's house with me for the Christmas party. Then you surprised them just a couple months ago with a visit. You think he won't start putting all this together?"

The Christmas party. As if Jack could forget. Viv had worn some emerald-green dress that hugged every damn curve she owned, and that memory had haunted his dreams, sleeping and awake, ever since. He'd been her faux date so he could get inside and eavesdrop. Not that he thought some epic family secrets would be revealed, but he wasn't letting the opportunity pass him by…and he sure as hell wasn't letting another man take his place.

Jealousy was an unwelcome bastard.

"That was months ago," he told her. "Besides, I had a full beard then and my hair was longer. And when I approached them after, I didn't look like the same man. They have no clue. They know now I'm onto them, but they don't realize I was the guy at the party with you."

He often changed his appearance, even in minor ways, because the average person didn't look beneath the surface. With all the people milling about, Jack was confident nobody would remember him from the Christmas party...not when he'd been overshadowed by Vivianna's beauty. He'd also been sure to make himself scarce the times she'd chatted with the key players. This had certainly not been his first time sneaking around and altering his identity.

"And what are you going to say?" she demanded in a harsh whisper. "You can't very well ask him to spill all his illegal doings."

Jack wondered if she had any idea that her eyes widened when she grew angry, that one of her brows arched higher than the other.

"I've done this a long time," he assured her. "Trust me."

Viv closed her eyes, reaching up to rub her forehead. Glancing at his watch, he was surprised to see that they'd been at this for quite a while. Katie had been asleep for over an hour, and judging by the dark circles under her eyes, Jack guessed it had been a while since Viv had actually had a restful night's sleep herself.

"Go in my office and lie down."

Viv lifted her head, smoothing her hair behind her ear. Her braid had started unraveling, giving her that sexy, tousled look. As if she needed to look sexier.

"You're exhausted and she's asleep. I promise I'll come get you when she wakes."

Because he'd have no clue what to do with a baby, and attempting to learn now would not be wise for the sake of his sanity.

Viv shook her head. "I'm fine."

Not surprising that she refused, but he wasn't about to let her win this fight...or any other, for that matter.

"Thirty minutes," he stated. "The couch is more than comfortable."

"You're speaking from experience?" She tipped her head to the side, knowing very well he slept in his office on occasion.

"I'm not asking, Viv. I'm telling you."

She rubbed her temples, as she'd done several times in the past twenty minutes, and Jack wondered if her head ached from her hair being pulled back or because she'd been staring at her computer screen.

Pulling her braid over her shoulder, she reached up and jerked the rubber band out. After threading her fingers through the strands to loosen them, she gave her head a shake. There was no way he could take his eyes off her now. The simple move was just as sultry and seductive as a striptease. All that long, rich hair spilling down her back, the groan that slipped through her lips had his own body stirring. Again.

"Viv."

Damn, that had come out like a growl.

Her eyes snapped to his. They'd worked countless hours in her office, but this was the first time he'd locked the main door so they wouldn't be interrupted. This was also the first time they'd closed her office door, but that was for Katie's sake. Still, being so confined with Vivianna, knowing the crackling sexual tension wasn't going anywhere, Jack was having a difficult time focusing.

He rubbed his index finger against his thumb, practically feeling all that hair wrapped around his hand as he tugged on it...from behind.

Raking a hand down his face, Jack finally came to his feet. "Actually, head on home. We're not getting anywhere, and I'm going to call Braden anyway and arrange a meeting."

Viv continued to look up at him. All that hair spread around her, those midnight eyes wide... His body stirred again.

"Why are you angry?"

*More like sexually frustrated.*

Jack shoved his hands in his pockets. "I'm not angry with you. There's so much at stake here and I refuse to let those bastards get the best of me."

Katie made a whimpering sound and Jack realized he hadn't even tried to keep his voice down. Viv's gaze darted in the baby's direction, then back to Jack.

"They won't," she told him. "But don't be so hellbent on destruction that you don't find the truth."

"What the hell does that mean?" he demanded in a harsh whisper.

Viv circled her desk to stand before him. "I'm just as eager to learn what happened to the Parkers as you are, but what if the O'Sheas truly had nothing to do with their murders?"

This was the first Jack had heard her even mention any doubts. Where were they coming from?

Viv smoothed her hair behind her shoulders. "Listen, I know you and the Feds want to nail the O'Sheas. I understand. I just really don't know that they had anything to do with that night."

Jack gritted his teeth. "If you're getting soft because you're working there—"

"I'm not getting soft." As if to prove her point, she tipped her chin and narrowed her eyes. "If anything, I'm getting to know them a bit better, and I can honestly say I just don't see it."

Jack couldn't believe this. He threw his hands in the air. "Most criminals don't go around with a sign announcing their offenses. Of course they're going to be friendly toward you so you're not apprehensive. And why the sudden change of heart? You never questioned my suspicions before."

She said nothing, just kept staring at him as if she wasn't sure how to respond...or as if she knew something he didn't. His radar wasn't often off the mark. Why would Viv come to the defense of such seasoned criminals?

"Did one of them threaten you?" he murmured, taking a step closer to her.

"What? No, of course not."

She gripped his elbow and squeezed. A simple gesture any friend would use when trying to get his attention. Still, the touch from Viv was anything but friendly...at least in his own mind.

"Listen, I'm just saying they definitely had their share of, shall we say, questionable transactions in the past." Viv offered him a sweet smile. "But with Braden in charge now, I know they are trying to keep things on the up and up."

Viv clearly wanted to see the best in this family. Perhaps it was because Laney was pregnant and Viv felt protective—one woman to another. Jack wasn't quite sure, but he'd done this work long enough that he refused to be sidetracked by the family's sudden need to walk on the right side of the law.

He reached for Viv's hand on his arm. Sliding it between his, he held her still, ignoring the way her eyes widened in surprise.

"I need you, Viv." In ways he couldn't even let himself believe. "You're my eyes and ears on the inside. You can't get caught up in this family when we're on the brink of shutting them down."

When she trembled, Jack gripped her hand tighter. She closed her eyes and pulled in a breath. Black lashes fanned out against her tanned skin. What was she so worried about?

"Is it because Laney is expecting?" he asked. "Is that what has you upset?"

Viv shook her head, lifting her lids to meet his

eyes. "No. Well, that does bother me, but I just worry not everything is as it seems."

"Is there something you need to tell me?"

Katie belted out a cry, which had Viv jerking her hand away and heading toward the baby. And just like that the moment was gone. What was Viv hiding? He turned and saw that she had entered her comfort zone as she wrapped her arms around Katie and swayed back and forth.

Viv's hair lay in waves down her back, shifting as she moved. She seemed to be humming in an attempt to sooth Katie's cries. Jack watched, wondering again why Viv had never pursued a family of her own. Maybe it was time he dug a little deeper into his assistant's personal life. After all, she was so determined to dive into his.

Days off were absolutely glorious. To have a day off from both jobs was even more splendid. Viv actually welcomed lounging in her pj's and getting caught up on housework. She'd gladly take wielding a toilet wand over volleying back and forth between a rumored mob family and the sexy boss she was hiding the truth from.

Katie crawled behind her as they headed down the hallway. With the baby still in her footed pajamas, her knees would occasionally slip on the hardwood, but she'd push herself right back up and continue on.

Viv didn't want to think about how she'd bounce back once this case wrapped up. Eventually Jack would learn the truth, in turn he'd hate her and at best she'd be fired. The fact she'd kept something so personal, so life altering from Jack would tear him apart. Plus, on top of the inevitable, the O'Sheas would likely learn she'd been spying. And Katie would find her forever home.

Viv pushed the negative thoughts away before they could consume her.

"Up, up, up."

Glancing over her shoulder, Viv laughed at Katie, who now sat at the end of the hall outside her bedroom. With her arms extended, she wiggled her little fingers back and forth and continued to demand, "Up."

Just as she started back down the hall to get Katie, Viv's cell chimed from the kitchen. She quickly scooped Katie up and played airplane as she ran the short distance to the galley-style kitchen. Braden's number lit up, instantly giving Viv's heart a few extra beats.

The new family patriarch for the O'Sheas had never been anything but kind to her, but she still worried at the random call. It wasn't typical of him to contact her when she was off, and with everything going on, she certainly didn't want to draw attention to herself.

Katie pulled on Viv's loose ponytail as she swiped her finger across the screen. "Hello?"

"Vivianna. I need you to come in to the office early on Tuesday."

That stern voice boomed through the line, reminding her of her father. Len Smith never let his children get out of line, except when Viv had wanted to leave home and live in a big city. But that was not a subject she wanted to think about right now.

"Of course," she replied, tipping her head when Katie reached for the cell. "Is one hour early enough?"

"That will be fine. The FBI needs to question all employees again." Braden blew out a sigh, as if echoing her own feelings. Fear also crawled up her spine, causing shivers. "It's a nuisance, but necessary to get them to back off. I apologize for putting you out. You've been an exemplary employee."

Well, either he didn't suspect her of anything or he was a really great actor trying to trap her.

"It's no bother at all," she replied. Katie lunged for the phone once more and Viv eased her back down to the floor. "I don't mind answering more questions."

Katie grabbed hold of Viv's plaid pajama bottoms and started her chant once again. "Up, up, up."

Braden laughed. "Sounds like you're busy, so I won't keep you."

The O'Sheas might be ruthless and known for their less-than-legal business dealings, but nobody could ever say they weren't a loving family. Family meant everything to them. And with Braden's wife and sister expecting babies, he apparently was in tune with little ones.

"I'll be there at eight on Tuesday," she told him, smiling down at Katie, who continued to tug, her tiny chin now quivering. "See you then."

She'd kept her voice steady, she hoped, while talking to him, but a new worry crept in. What if the

FBI had found something? The Feds knew she was a plant; Jack was very thorough with keeping his contacts informed. Still, if they were questioning the whole office, maybe they were about to crack this case.

And then what? What would Jack do? The journal was completely personal, so there was no need for the Feds to know about it at all. But she was the only living person who knew the truth. It was her moral duty to tell him, whether the case was blown open or not.

Katie started fussing, rubbing her eyes and biting down hard on her gums. Viv set the phone back on the counter and reached for her. It was getting later in the day, but Katie had been up nearly all night with teething pain. Viv would give anything if those teeth would just pop through and let Katie have some rest. Poor thing was turning one in a week and Viv wanted to plan a fun celebration, even if it was just the two of them.

"It's all right, sweetheart." Viv ran her hand up and down Katie's back as she headed toward the nursery. "Let's rock a bit and see if we can get you to rest."

Three hours, no sleep and an empty bottle of pain reliever later, Viv needed reinforcements. The bottle of medicine had only one dose left when she'd pulled it from the cabinet, but thankfully, she kept a spare in the diaper bag.

With Katie on her hip, Viv frantically searched her apartment. Where on earth could it be? She always kept it right by the front door so this didn't happen.

Katie's screams were getting worse and Viv's frustration level was soaring. How could she be so irresponsible and misplace the bag with the backup medicine in it? She'd put her spare bottle in the bag when she took Katie to the office yesterday and…

*Oh, no.* Viv's heart sank. The diaper bag was at the office. She'd completely forgotten it in her haste to get out of the confined space with Jack.

She could throw on clothes and run to the drugstore two blocks away, but she truly hated to take Katie out in this weather. She glanced at the clock hanging above her bookshelf and noted that it was much later than she'd thought. She really had only one option if there was any hope of sleep tonight.

# Six

Jack felt like a complete fool. His instincts had gotten him through combat; he'd managed to make enough business deals in the past decade to make him a millionaire; he spoke Italian and Portuguese and owned homes in both countries. Yet as he stood outside Viv's apartment door with diaper bag in hand, along with a sack of extra items from the store, he cursed under his breath.

He should've just brought the bag Viv had requested and not gone the extra mile. The last thing he needed was her reading too much into his actions. He was having a hard enough time justifying them to himself. He'd come damn close to kissing her in her office yesterday so he needed to calm down and reassess exactly what he needed to focus on…and it wasn't his assistant.

A middle-aged woman walked by and stopped at the next door. She threw him a soft smile, causing her eyes to wrinkle in the corners.

"You're here for Vivianna?" she asked.

Jack nodded. "You must be Martha."

He'd never met the babysitter before, but he knew she lived just on the other side of Viv. Jack shifted the diaper and drugstore bags into one hand and stepped forward to take Martha's bag of groceries.

"Let me," he offered, not letting her argue. "I'll carry them inside."

"But you have your own load."

Jack flashed her a smile. "Then you better unlock your door so I can go in and set yours down. My mother raised a gentleman."

She fished out her key and threw a glance over her shoulder as she turned the knob. "I like you. Are you here to take Viv out? That girl never gets out except to work."

Jack secured the large brown grocery bag against his chest as he followed Martha into her apartment, which was the same layout as Viv's. Martha decorated quite a bit differently, though. There wasn't a shelf or stationary surface that didn't have a knick-knack on it. The porcelain cats, ducks, random shot glasses from around the world…there was just so much to take in at once. How the hell did anyone watch a child here? Breakables were everywhere.

"I'm returning the diaper bag she left at work,"

Jack finally replied, once he got past the chaos of the place.

Martha motioned for him to set the bag on the dining table. "That's a shame. I was hoping some fine-looking young man was going to take her out on the town. I'd gladly watch Katie, if that were the case."

The naughty twinkle in the woman's eye had him inching toward the door. The last thing he needed was a meddling neighbor trying to play Cupid. He was getting along just fine on his own.

Who said money didn't buy happiness? He was happy, damn it.

When this was all over, he decided, he wouldn't vacation at his villa in Italy. He was buying a whole new house for a getaway. He'd always loved the beauty of Amsterdam. Maybe he'd go there and look into real estate.

"I'll let her know you're available." Jack started through the open door, but the woman wasn't done with him yet.

"The weather is getting bad out there." She wiggled her brows. "If you need to stay for a bit, just have Viv run Katie over."

Was this lady for real? Jack merely smiled with a nod and got the hell out. That was the babysitter? Jack needed to have a talk with Viv about this. Not that he had any say over whom she preferred to have babysit, and Katie sure as hell wasn't his kid, but Martha seemed a bit too eager to get a man alone with Viv.

How many other men had she tried to set Viv up with?

The thought irritated Jack as he pounded on her door. He had no right to be jealous, but damn it, he couldn't help where his thoughts instantly went. The idea of some faceless bastard—

The door jerked open. It took Jack a moment to fully assess everything before him. Viv's hair was half up, half down…and not in a stylish way. More like Katie had yanked on it in a fit kind of way.

Gone was her typical pencil skirt and silk blouse. She'd donned plaid pants—were those flannel?— and a long-sleeved T-shirt that was a bit damp in the chest region. And she wasn't wearing a bra. Maybe having Katie stay next door with the crazy neighbor was the safest option, after all.

"Thank God you're here." Viv blew out an exhausted breath. "She's been screaming for the past fifteen minutes. Sorry to bother you, but I figured you'd still be at the office this late."

The screamer in question turned from Viv's shoulder to look straight at Jack. Her little eyes were red and puffy, and drool covered her chin. Her blond curls were in disarray. The two females before him looked as if they'd been through a battle.

Jack stepped in and immediately put the diaper bag on the table just inside the door. Without asking, because he recalled from the last time, he reached into the front pocket and pulled out the pain reliever.

Katie let out a cry, and Viv grabbed the bottle from his hand. "I can't thank you enough. I really didn't want to get her out in this weather, and I can't believe I left the bag at the office. What kind of foster parent am I?"

She struggled with the lid and holding a fussy baby. Jack eased the medicine from her hands and twisted it open. "You're the best foster parent."

Tears welled in Viv's eyes. "She's been miserable and I couldn't do anything to help."

He understood that helpless feeling all too well.

As Viv administered the medicine, Jack shrugged out of his coat and hung it over the back of one of two kitchenette chairs. Then he returned to the accent table and started pulling things from the drugstore sack.

"What are you doing?" Viv asked.

*Feeling like a fool at the moment.*

"I didn't want you to run out of pain reliever tonight, so I brought a few backups."

He stacked the various boxes on the table, because he didn't know which brand was the best and had bought two boxes of each.

"A few?" she asked with a slight laugh. "That will last me forever. Maybe you should be a foster parent. Clearly, you plan ahead better than I do."

She had no clue that associating the word *parent* with him was literally like a knife to his chest. She didn't know, because he'd never told her.

When Viv swiped at her damp eyes, Jack nearly reached for her. And what good would come from that? What did he intend to do once he touched her? Console her? Tell her everything would be all right?

He sucked at consoling, to be honest. He wanted to, damn it. She made him want to try. He hated that she obviously felt inadequate and second-guessed herself.

Katie whimpered a bit more and Viv patted her back, bouncing softly in an attempt to calm her. "I'm sorry you had to stop here on your way home," Viv told him, then blew a stray strand of hair from her eyes. "I'm even sorrier I'm a complete wreck."

"You're not a wreck. You look like a woman who's putting the needs of a child first." Which made her even sexier. "Never apologize for caring."

Viv kissed Katie on the forehead and smoothed back her unruly curls. "I just hate to see her in pain. Teething is no joke. We were up most of last night, then she was fine this morning and I managed to get my cleaning done."

He might not be able to do much, but Jack knew of one thing that would hopefully put a smile on her face. He reached for the last item in the bag.

Viv gasped as he held up her favorite candy. "I think I love you."

Jack froze. Viv's eyes widened. "I mean, thank you," she quickly added. "You don't know how low my stash was running, and these are the name brand. I always buy the generic."

Yeah, he'd seen the empty bags in her office, which was just one of the reasons he wanted her to have the real thing.

Jack tore the package open and crossed toward her

kitchen. He dumped the candy into her glass bowl and tossed the empty sack.

"I met your neighbor," he commented, leaning back against the counter. "Does she always try to set you up with a booty call?"

Viv's eyes widened. Her hand, which she had been rubbing up and down Katie's spine, stilled. "Excuse me?"

Shrugging, Jack went on. "She was all too eager for me to let you know she'd watch Katie if I wanted to take you out, or if we wanted to stay in, since the roads are getting bad."

Viv closed her eyes and wrinkled her nose. "Please tell me she didn't really say that."

Jack bit the inside of his cheek to suppress his grin. "Do you think I would make that up?"

When she finally opened her eyes, she looked everywhere but directly at him. Vivianna was sexy as hell and adorable all at the same time…and that invisible string pulling him toward her kept getting shorter and shorter. There wasn't a damn thing he could do to stop it. He hadn't felt the stirrings of desire for another woman in years.

"She's tried to set me up on dates so many times, but this is a first."

Viv shifted Katie in her arms. Apparently, the medicine had started kicking in, because the infant had one fist in her mouth and was playfully tugging Viv's fallen hair with her free hand.

"In her defense, she was married to her high school sweetheart for forty years. He passed from a heart attack a couple of years ago." Viv moved into the living area and started to put Katie in her Pack 'n Play. Having other ideas, Katie merely clung to her. "She's always looking for someone for me because she thinks I'm unhappy alone."

Jack navigated around the half wall separating the kitchen from the family room. "And are you unhappy alone?"

Finally, those dark eyes met his. "I'm not alone. I have Katie."

He came to a stop within a foot of her. "And when she's gone? Will you still be happy?"

Viv tipped her chin. "I'm always sad to see my foster kids leave. Saying goodbye to Katie will be harder to deal with because I'm so close to the story. But if you're asking if I need a man in my life to make me happy, the answer is no."

"What does make you happy?"

Why was he asking? Jack wondered. He should get his coat on and get the hell out. The roads weren't getting any better and…what other reasoning did he need? He was getting too cozy with his assistant.

"Right now?" She raised her brows and smiled. "A shower. If you'd watch Katie for me for just five minutes, I will put in all the extra hours you want and you won't even have to pay me."

Watch Katie? Jack would rather hand over his no-limit credit card and send Viv on a trip to Rodeo Drive. Not because he didn't like children. Quite the opposite. But there was that fear that had been ingrained in him a decade ago. He'd been so hyped up on the idea of becoming a father, and then when that dream vanished, he'd forced himself to shut down that side of his mind.

"It's okay." Viv shook her head with a wave of her hand when he remained silent. "I just appreciate you bringing the bag and all the backups, especially the candy. Having her medicine is clearly more important than my hygiene at the moment."

He was such a jerk. Here he was worried about his fears, when Viv was constantly putting everyone's needs ahead of her own. From being an incredible foster mother to Katie, to working at—no, excelling at—two jobs because of him, the woman was a marvel. And all she wanted was a damn shower.

"Go shower. I'll watch her."

Viv's eyes widened in surprise, mimicking his own feelings. The offer was out of his mouth before he could talk himself out of it, but he wasn't sorry. The second her shock wore off, her entire face softened and her smile warmed something deep within him…something he'd thought he buried with his wife and unborn child.

He thought Viv might argue or tell him not to worry about it, but she quickly handed Katie over and muttered a thank-you as she dashed down the hallway.

Gripping the child beneath her arms, Jack looked into her baby blue eyes. The irony that she'd lost her parents and he'd lost his own child was not wasted on him. But it wasn't like he was going to be in Katie's life permanently. Still, holding her didn't make him miserable. In some strange way he couldn't explain, having her in his arms was rather therapeutic.

Katie smiled as drool ran down her chin and dripped onto his hand. Even that didn't turn him off. When he tucked her against his side, he felt a bit awkward. But the way she kept her eyes on him, as if she fully trusted him, had his heart stirring.

He hoped like hell Viv stuck to that five-minute plan because he wasn't sure how much longer his emotions or his sanity could hold out against the power of this innocent infant.

Viv felt human again. She'd managed a quick shower, hair washing included, and she'd brushed her teeth. She'd been mortified that Jack had to see her so...so blah. There had been no way around it, though. She'd needed the bag and she'd known he would be at the office.

The fact that he'd brought her the name-brand candy had her wondering if he was reaching out to her on a personal level. Obviously, but why?

Viv wasn't going to dig too deep into this, because even if Jack was trying to become personal, she was harboring a colossal secret. Pulling in a deep breath as she tugged her tank top over her head, Viv realized this case might never be solved. Would she have to hide the truth from Jack forever? But he deserved to know, even though it might ruin his quest for justice...and her chance at a deeper connection with him.

Worry coiled low in her belly. She didn't like secrets and she'd never been a liar before.

Well, until she became a spy for Jack and started working for the O'Sheas. Her moral compass had never been so screwed up in her life.

As she came down the hall, she wondered how long she should give herself before she told him. Each day that passed only added more layers to her guilt. But before she could give herself a time line, the sight in the living room stopped her every thought.

Jack was the sexiest man she'd ever met and reduced her insides to mush every time he entered the room. But seeing him cuddling a sleeping baby might just be the ovary buster.

Nestled in the crook of his arm, Katie seemed perfectly content to catch some much-needed rest against Jack's broad chest. And Viv was a tad jealous.

"I'm sorry," she whispered as she crossed the room. "I tried to hurry."

Jack's eyes met hers, then traveled down her body. Every part of her tingled just as if he'd touched her. Perhaps she should've put on more than a pair of sleep shorts and a tank, but she'd been in a rush and grabbed the first thing she came across.

"She was out almost as soon as you walked away," he stated, glancing back down at Katie. "Now what do I do with her?"

Inching closer, Viv brushed against his arm as she stood on her tiptoes to look down on Katie. Such a precious little girl, one who trusted so easily. Viv didn't want Jack to leave just yet, but she wasn't sure if he wanted to continue to hold the sleeping baby.

"Are you hungry?" Viv asked, looking back up at him. "I could make dinner for us. But if you want to get home, I totally understand. Nothing I make would compare to Tilly's cooking."

A smile flirted around the corners of his mouth. "I can stay. She isn't cooking tonight. I actually threatened to give her the week off, because she's about as subtle as your neighbor and wanted you to come back for dinner...and breakfast."

Viv couldn't help the images of all the possibilities surrounding that scenario that popped into her head. But she'd never spend the night in Jack's bed—especially after she revealed the truth.

"Then maybe Martha and Tilly shouldn't meet," she stated as she moved around him. "Would you mind holding the baby for a bit longer while I get dinner ready?"

Jack's lips thinned as he stared at Katie. "Not one bit."

There was a sadness to his tone, one Viv wanted to explore but had no right to. She had bigger problems... like cooking a dinner that a millionaire would find appealing. She had a feeling microwave mac 'n cheese wouldn't make the greatest impression.

Viv tried to block out the image of Jack holding a baby in her living room while she made dinner. There was so much wrapped in this moment—fear, hope, nervousness, sexual tension. All she could do now was concentrate on cooking. Later, she'd sort out her emotions—and decide when to come clean to Jack about his birth father.

# Seven

Jack held Katie while Viv ate her simple meal of hamburger, baked potato and salad. She had protested, but Jack had insisted, gentleman that he was. Or maybe he'd just taken pity on her after witnessing her tears and frustration earlier. She was so grateful he was here—not that she should get used to having him around.

Once she was done, Viv crossed to the living room, where Jack sat on her hand-me-down sofa. He looked so out of place with that designer suit, groomed hair and a baby sleeping across his chest. Still, he looked perfectly at home, too. How cruel of her heart to cling to such a ridiculous fantasy.

Viv eased the still-sleeping baby from his arms so he could get up and go eat.

"I never dreamed she'd sleep this long," Viv muttered. "I'm just going to lay her down in her room. I'll be right back."

Viv had gotten his plate ready and poured him a glass of iced tea, which was all she had unless he wanted whole milk or water. Definitely nothing like the dinner he'd served her at his house. But she wasn't ashamed of how she lived. She wasn't a billionaire, but she rocked the thousandaire title pretty well.

As long as she had enough funds to keep fostering and caring for children who had nobody else, she didn't care how padded her bank account was. A trip to Tahiti would be nice, but was definitely not a necessity.

Viv took her time laying Katie down in the white crib she'd found in a secondhand shop and repainted. The yellow bedding was cheery, yet calm, quite the opposite of Viv's nerves.

The stress of the secret was weighing on her. The fear of the unknown, the future, scared her more than anything. But she had to remain quiet for now…all the more motivation to help Jack clear up this case sooner rather than later.

Darkness had long since settled in, causing the tiny night-light to kick on in Katie's room. Viv gave the baby one last glance before pulling in a deep breath and tiptoeing away. After being up all night and agitated all afternoon, Katie would sleep until morning, she hoped.

Viv backed out of the room, pulling the door

closed. Jack's strong hands gripped her arms just as she was about to turn.

"Sorry." His whispered word by the side of her cheek sent shivers through her. His firm touch on her bare arms nearly had her leaning back against his chest. "I didn't want you to trip over me."

Viv turned, but Jack didn't take a step back. So close. He was so close, yet with just the soft glow from the kitchen light and the small lamp in the living room, she could barely make out his expression.

"I need to get going," he told her. "I just wanted to thank you for dinner. Tilly is the only one who cooks for me, so this was a nice change."

Viv refused to believe a man who'd traveled the globe, both for business and pleasure, was impressed by a meal she'd thrown together.

"Actually, before you go, could we just talk?"

She didn't want him to leave.

Jack tipped his head. "I don't think that's a good idea."

Viv stepped away from the door so she didn't wake Katie. "Why isn't it a good idea?"

He moved in front of her, raking a hand over his hair, ruffling it, reminding her of the unkempt way he'd worn it when they'd first met. The man could seriously shave his head or grow his hair long and still have just as much sex appeal.

His eyes narrowed. "Exploring this tension between us isn't a good idea."

Wait...what? He thought she was about to bring up the chemistry between them?

First of all, she wasn't that brave. Second, he clearly thought of her in that way or it wouldn't be an issue. Part of her wanted to jump up and down, but the realistic side remembered the damning journal in her bedroom.

She'd just wanted him to stay so she'd have some company. Okay, that was a lie. She wanted him here so they could talk about something that maybe wasn't only work. Perhaps if he would just slide into personal territory even once, maybe he'd see she was more than an assistant. She was a woman with a desire for her boss.

"I was—"

"I don't like tension in my work space," Jack continued. His broad shoulders blocked the light from the living area.

"And you think there's a problem between us?"

Why did she suddenly sound husky, like some seductress? She certainly wasn't trying to seduce him. Not that it would be a hardship.

"I think you drive me out of my mind." Jack took a half step closer, towering over her and doing nothing to slow her rapid heartbeat. "I blame myself for my thoughts, but I blame you for making me want things I have no business wanting."

Viv's breath caught in her throat. He'd never made such bold statements before. She'd caught him looking, but he'd never, ever been this audacious. She'd be lying if she denied the sudden thrill of knowing he couldn't ignore his feelings. All this time she'd thought he was made of stone. Clearly, this man was all flesh and blood. And sending her smoldering looks from mere inches away.

"I'm not trying to do anything to you," she murmured. "I'm attracted to you, but I know you're my boss and that's a line we can't cross, even if you were interested in me that way."

Jack muttered a curse, took a step forward and had her pinned between his hard chest and the wall. He propped one hand next to her head as he leaned in.

"*If* I was interested?" he repeated with a laugh of disbelief. "Do I look like a man who isn't interested, Viv?"

She bit the inside of her cheek. Treading this unfamiliar territory was not how she thought the evening would go down. She needed to tell him about the journal... That would squelch any interest he had. But now wasn't the time.

Jack placed his other hand on the opposite side of her head. He didn't touch her, but there was barely enough air moving between them in that miniscule gap.

"Just one taste," he whispered. "You should stop me now."

He didn't give her an option to answer before his mouth covered hers...not that she would've protested. She'd waited too long for this moment and she was going to savor each and every touch.

But the kiss remained his only touch. He didn't rush, didn't force. He didn't need to. The slow, sensual way his mouth moved over hers instantly had her wanting more.

He lifted his head slightly, just enough to change the angle before capturing her lips beneath his again. Viv couldn't hold back. She didn't have the will-power Jack apparently possessed.

She lifted her hands to his shoulders as he nipped at her lips. When he shifted slightly, bringing their bodies flush against each other, Viv let out a groan. If he'd offered to take her to her room right now, she wouldn't have objected.

Jack left her mouth to trail kisses along her jaw-line. Before she could stop herself, his name escaped her lips in a whispered plea.

He stilled beneath her touch and slowly lifted his head. When their eyes connected, there was enough of a glow for her to see he was done. His pained expression was back, the torment he inflicted on himself so evident from his thinned lips and the creases between his brows.

"Jack," she muttered once again. "You don't have to stop."

His hands fell to his sides as he took a step back. A chill enveloped her and she knew that self-erected wall was back in place.

"I need to go."

She didn't get a word in before he turned on his heel. In moments, the front door opened and closed, leaving her feeling even worse than before the kiss.

Viv slid down the wall, pulled her knees to her chest and dropped her head. Why did he have to kiss her? If she'd known he was going to have instant regrets, she would've preferred he leave her alone.

Now all she could feel were his lips. He'd touched her nowhere else, but her entire body still hummed.

And from his reaction, she knew he would never touch her again.

Tears burned in her eyes. She'd practically inhaled her boss, then begged him not to stop. How the hell would she ever show her face at work tomorrow?

"If you have nothing to hide, then meeting me won't be a problem."

Jack's gloved hand gripped his steering wheel. Frustration rolled through him from all angles, especially concerning that kiss he'd experienced an hour ago. He could still taste her.

But now his anger shifted from himself to Ryker Barrett. This was one tough guy to crack, but Jack was tougher. He wasn't intimidated by the mob family's thug.

"Meeting you would be a waste of my time," Ryker replied.

"On the contrary," Jack countered. "You can't dodge the fact you all are the key suspects in the Parkers' murders."

"Nothing to dodge. Do you honestly believe we'd steal the items we wanted to auction? Pretty hard to pull that off, even for us."

Jack hated this man. Hated the way he blew off the fact the Feds were swarming all around the O'Sheas. Either they were that arrogant or they truly had nothing to hide. Jack refused to believe this family had turned so lily-white after Patrick's passing.

The patriarch was notorious for getting deals done, no matter the cost. He'd been careful, had the right people in his back pocket and had never even gotten so much as a parking ticket.

And Jack would be the one to bring them all down.

"Come by the coffee shop next to my office tomorrow at eight," Ryker finally grunted.

Jack hung up and tossed the phone onto the leather passenger seat. Snow continued to fall and here he sat outside Viv's apartment. He'd battled whether to go back in and apologize, then he'd opted to call Ryker and set up a meeting instead. He wasn't worried about meeting with him, especially in a public place. The O'Sheas—and their henchman—were playing it smart now, anyway. They knew they were being watched and didn't want to bring more attention to themselves.

Jack would start with Ryker, then move to Braden, Mac, anyone who would talk and give Jack the lead he needed to crack this damn case.

It was getting late and he still had a call to make with one of his clients in the UK, to go over some security detail he was sending a team to cover. A simple job that would pay an easy seven figures. It was the one aspect of his life where he could maintain control and keep his sanity intact.

Because kissing the hell out of Viv had cost him everything.

He never showed weakness, never let his guard down, but he had done both with her. He'd gotten too damn cozy holding Katie while waiting on Viv to cook dinner. This wasn't some suburban family setting, yet it had sure felt that way to him.

Beyond the whole domestic feel of the evening, Viv had come out from her shower smelling like lilacs and innocence. They were both damn lucky all he did was kiss her. He'd at least held on to that last thread of control by not putting his hands all over her…but damn, how he'd wanted to.

She was his assistant. The only woman, other than Tilly, he'd let into his life on any level since his wife had passed.

Jack knew his wife would've wanted him to move on. That wasn't the issue. The issue was the pain he'd gone through when he'd lost her. Every single damn day since her murder, he'd had to live with the fact that he hadn't been there to protect her. Did he want to open himself up to even the slightest risk of that happening again?

No. He had business dealings all over the world, clients who demanded his full attention. There was no woman who would understand, not even Viv. Besides, he was a much different man than he'd been a decade ago. Life had blindsided him and left him to pick up each shattered piece. He hadn't even had the energy to put all the shards back together. Instead he'd opted for a fresh start, completely revamping his future goals.

Never once had seducing his assistant been on his list.

Jack put his SUV in gear and pulled from the

curb. He had to put some distance between him and Viv. Had to get his head on straight so he could come out on top during tomorrow's meeting. And he had to forget the way Viv had kissed him back with total abandon and want. Because he knew if he went back up to her apartment to apologize now, they'd end up taking a step he wasn't sure he'd ever be ready for.

# Eight

She hadn't had a good glass of wine in so long, but Viv was rewarding herself tonight. Katie had fallen asleep without incident. Martha said there had been no issues during the day, and Katie had two teeth popping through. Viv nearly wept with relief at the sight of those little white points.

She'd gone into O'Shea's earlier in the day. Even though it was Saturday, they were getting ready for the spring auction and there was a constant stream of data to be inputted.

Viv had left the office early and done some birthday shopping for Katie. She was turning only one and would never remember this time in her life, but Viv wanted to make the day special. She'd never had a foster child at birthday time before and she may have gone a bit overboard. Her credit card had definitely taken a hit, but she didn't care.

Once Katie had gone down, Viv had relaxed with a bubble bath. The lavender lotion she'd applied afterward had instantly calmed the rest of her nerves.

She hadn't heard from Jack since he'd kissed her and bolted out the door. His silence spoke volumes, though. For a man who checked in with her almost hourly, he'd gone off the grid, most likely to analyze his actions. Knowing Jack, he was going to come back with some quick, stern apology and expect to move on like nothing had happened. He would shut down once again if she didn't do something to make him realize that the kiss had not been a mistake.

If it had been, she wouldn't still be tingling and reliving every glorious detail.

Viv settled back against her pile of pillows, propped her feet on her bed and reached for the book on her nightstand. Armed with a glass of wine and a good novel, she didn't care what went on for the next hour or so. She was taking this time for herself.

With the snow blowing around outside, being cozy in her apartment was the perfect setting for getting lost in a good book. Unfortunately, she'd started this one so long ago she'd have to start over to refresh her memory.

Viv had just opened the hardback when she heard a thump. She glanced to the video monitor screen on her nightstand. Katie hadn't moved one inch since being laid down. Viv strained to hear another sound, figuring it must be one of her neighbors.

Just as she dismissed the noise, she heard it. Sounded like someone was at her front door. quickly set her glass and book on the nightstand, grabbed her phone and the monitor and tiptoed across the hall to Katie's bedroom. If someone was trying to get in, she wanted to be in the same room as the baby.

Her building had security, but nothing like the fingerprint scanner at Jack's office and his home. Her heart beat too fast as possible scenarios flooded her mind. Was someone trying to get in? Was this related to the case she was working on from both sides?

It was too late for visitors and the only people who ever dropped by her place were Jack and Martha. Viv didn't figure either of them would be attempting to get in to her apartment.

Viv heard a creak, very faint. She couldn't just open the door and look, because if someone was there, they could hurt her and take Katie. Right now, Viv needed to stay with the baby.

She dialed Jack and willed him to answer and not still be sulking about their intense kiss.

He answered on the second ring. "Viv."

"I think someone is in my apartment," she whispered. She kept her eyes glued to the crack beneath the bedroom door, praying she wouldn't see a shadow.

"Don't move," he said, his tone suddenly alert. "I'll be there in five minutes."

In other words, a lifetime.

"Don't hang up," he told her. "Keep this line open while I drive so I know you're okay."

Beneath the bold, firm command, Viv caught an underlying sense of fear.

"Don't be reckless," she whispered. "The roads are—"

"Damn the roads," he growled. "Talk to me. Where are you and Katie in the apartment?"

"I came into her room."

She heard another faint thump and squeezed her eyes shut. She'd never been one to rely on someone else to get her out of a jam, but this was different. Fear gripped her as she stood by the crib, clutching the phone and watching the door. She'd at least turned the simple lock when she'd come in.

"Viv."

"I'm here."

"Don't talk anymore," he ordered. "I'm almost at your street."

Still minutes from getting in to her apartment. But just knowing he was close, knowing he was on the other end of the line, was a comfort.

Thankfully, Katie slept on, unaware of any turmoil.

Viv hadn't heard anything in the past couple minutes, but she wasn't ready to step out of the room and leave Katie yet.

"I just parked and I'm heading inside."

He already knew the building code and the code to her apartment. Viv waited, hearing random clicks and footsteps through her cell phone.

He was in her building and she was going to be just fine. But was someone out there waiting for him?

"Be careful," she whispered.

Then she heard a few beeps seconds before her apartment door opened.

"The door was closed and I don't see anyone in here."

The heavy weight lifted from her shoulders as she tucked the monitor under her arm and quietly stepped from Katie's bedroom. Jack stood at the end of the hall, filling the opening with his broad shoulders. She'd never seen a more beautiful sight in all her life.

And it struck her that her first instinct had been to call him and not 911. Jack was the only protection, only security she wanted.

With the monitor and phone clutched to her chest, she moved on into her bedroom and dumped them on the bed. The wine and the book remained on the table where she'd left them what seemed like hours ago.

Wrapping her arms around her waist, she tipped her head down and drew in a shaky breath. Strong hands gripped her shoulders and Jack pulled her against his firm chest.

"You're fine now."

She nodded, afraid to speak. His heartbeat at her back was nearly as frantic as her own.

"Sorry I bothered you so late," she muttered.

"I would've been pissed had you not."

She turned, not caring how utterly unprofessional this entire scenario was, and wrapped her arms around his neck.

"Give me just a minute," she murmured against his chest. "I just…need to get my heart rate back under control."

When his arms circled her, tugging her tighter against him, Viv melted right into his embrace. The woodsy cologne he always used filled her senses. The warmth from his touch had her nerves settling. Just knowing she'd called and he'd beat feet to get here had her heart swelling.

"Thank you." Viv eased back to look up into his eyes. "I probably should've called 911, but I thought of you and then I heard another noise. I just dialed your number without thinking and didn't know who else to—"

Jack placed a finger over her lips. "I'm always your first call. Always."

Viv nodded, never taking her eyes off his. She noticed then that she wasn't the one trembling now. Every part of him, from his hand touching her face to his body pressed against hers, had a slight tremor.

Curling her fingers around his wrist, Viv pulled his hand away. "Are you all right?"

"Of course I am."

The words came out on a huff, as if she were asking an absurd question. But worry was etched all over his face. The drawn brows, the thin lips. Jack had been just as scared, maybe more, than she had been.

"You're shaking."

"Adrenaline." He kept her close, his gaze on her face. "It's not often I get a phone call after midnight unless it's business, and even then I'm expecting it."

She noticed then that this was quite possibly the first time she'd ever seen him sporting something other than an Italian-cut suit. He wore jeans and a long-sleeved black T-shirt. He hadn't even bothered with a coat.

And she was even more aware of how little she wore, considering she'd gotten ready for bed. Suddenly her silk tap shorts and matching pink tank seemed like nothing. The thin material was barely a barrier between them.

Viv took a step back, hating how her body cooled instantly once away from his touch. "Um…sorry you came for nothing. I think I'll be fine now."

Jack's eyes raked over her. "I'm not leaving."

Heart in her throat, Viv crossed her arms over her chest—the only defense she had, given the nearly sheer material and no bra. "It's fine, Jack. I'm sure it was a neighbor and my mind just played tricks on me. I'm sorry I dragged you out in this weather."

"Never apologize and never call me second when you need someone." He took a step forward, closing the gap between them. "I'm staying on the couch tonight."

"But—"

"I'm not asking your permission." He glanced around her bedroom, his eyes landing on the nightstand with her wine and book. "Pretend I'm not here."

Viv snorted. As if that were even a possibility.

Once again, he was visually sampling her—and he wasn't hiding the fact. Having Jack on her couch all night would ensure one thing...there was no way in hell she'd get one wink of sleep.

# Nine

Jack was used to sleeping in random places. The military had instilled that ability in him from the get-go. Then, when he'd started doing surveillance, he spent many nights holed up in his car or a van with video equipment. While he might have eight bedrooms, in his home here and villas in two other countries, he wasn't pampered and didn't need the finest accommodations. He was comfortable anywhere.

Or so he thought.

Viv's sofa smelled like flowers, like her. And he could possibly get beyond that, but every time he tried to close his eyes, images of her in that damn silky pajama number flooded his mind.

Hell, he didn't even need to close his eyes to see that glorious view.

And how much of a jerk was he, sitting here fantasizing about her, when she'd been scared out of her mind earlier. When she'd called him, Jack hadn't even thought. There hadn't been time. The fear in her tone, the way she whispered that she needed him, had absolutely gutted him…and thrown him back ten years.

Letting anyone else get hurt, or worse, on his watch again was not an option. Especially someone he cared about. And he did care about Viv—more than he would ever admit.

Jack dropped his head back against the cushion and stared into the darkness. Viv was only a few walls away, still wearing that outfit that dreams were made of. How much willpower did a man have?

Part of him wanted to ignore the fact that she was his assistant, and to go take what they both wanted. The boss part of him knew there would be no turning back—and the boundaries he'd so carefully constructed would be permanently blurred.

Did he really want to risk that for one night?

Before Jack could think too much, he came to his feet. Hell, yes, he wanted to risk it. If anything, he'd learned to take what he wanted out of life…and he wanted Vivianna Smith.

She'd stared at the same page, the same paragraph, for the past fifteen minutes. She'd downed her wine immediately, because she'd needed something to calm her nerves…nerves that had nothing to do with the scare she'd had earlier and everything to do with the man keeping guard in her living room.

That whole protective nature of his was such a turn-on, as if she needed more reasons to want him. So far the only flaw she'd discovered was his inability to let anyone behind the wall he'd erected around himself.

But after the way he'd kissed her, the way he'd looked at her and proved to be a white knight, Viv wasn't letting her desire go. She had to know if there was more passion in him where that came from.

Her mind made up, she set the book on the nightstand next to her empty glass. Just as she rose to her feet, there was a creak outside her bedroom. A second later, the door eased open.

Viv stood next to her bed, eyes locked on Jack filling her doorway. The small accent lamp on her nightstand was the only thing illuminating the space. Jack raked his gaze over her as he'd done earlier...as if he couldn't get enough. She was counting on just that.

"What took you so long?" she asked. "I was coming to you."

He stayed in the doorway, but Viv wasn't deterred. She knew he'd come this far and wasn't about to leave. She remained by the bed, because there was no way she was going to cross that space now. The next move was his.

"This is it," he murmured, stepping over the threshold. "Tonight has nothing to do with tomorrow."

If that's what he chose to believe, whatever. She knew better, but she wasn't about to argue, not when she was so turned on she was about ready to pounce on him.

"What changed your mind?"

He stalked closer, until they were toe to toe and she had to tilt her head to look into his eyes. "Does it matter?"

In the grand scheme of things maybe, but right this second? No.

Anticipation had her stomach quivering. Now that he was in her bedroom, Viv really wished he'd do something rather than stand so close with no contact. Throw her down on the bed, for starters.

Jack's fingertips traveled up her bare arms, across her collarbone, before slowly sliding the straps of her tank out of the way.

"Do you always wear sexy silk things to bed?" His eyes remained on the task of undressing her as he spoke.

"Yes."

He eased the thin material down until the tank pooled around her waist. Instinctively, her body arched, reacting to the cooler air and the anticipation of his touch. He was slowly killing her.

"If you don't move faster, I'm going to take over."

Jack's eyes darted to hers. "I've waited for this. I'm going to take in every single second."

He'd waited? For how long?

Before she could analyze his statement too much, Jack hooked his thumbs in the bunched material around her waist and slid everything lower. When he crouched down, she lifted one foot, then the other, until she was completely bared to him.

If any other man was at her feet, Viv would think him submissive, but she knew better with Jack. He was in control at all times.

Jack curled his fingers around her ankles, then pushed his way up her body, over her hips to the dip in her waist, until he was on his feet again. Viv let out a moan when he finally palmed her breasts.

"You're so responsive."

Now wouldn't be the time to tell him she'd never been this responsive to another man. She'd never ached for a man like this before. Viv wanted to see him, too, all of him. She reached for the hem of his shirt and jerked it up. Jack released her long enough to whip the garment over his head and toss it aside. Keeping his eyes locked on hers, he quickly rid himself of his jeans and boxer briefs, until he stood before her in all his glorious masculinity.

"I'm not—"

Her thoughts were lost as he snaked his arms around her waist and pulled her against his body. His mouth crashed down onto hers as if every shred of his control had snapped.

The backs of her knees hit the edge of her bed. Jack followed her down, never breaking away from her. The weight of his body pressing her into the duvet was a welcome sensation. She'd dreamed of this moment, never thinking he'd be in her bed. In her imagination they'd always been in one of the rooms of his grand home.

Jack pulled his lips from hers as he looked down into her eyes. He rested his elbows on either side of her head, smoothing her hair away from her face.

"Be sure."

Viv bent her knees, sliding her ankles around his waist and locking them behind his back. When he closed his eyes and pulled in a deep breath, she stilled. Realization hit her.

"You don't have protection, do you?" she asked.

He shook his head. "I clearly didn't plan this when I left."

"I don't keep anything here."

The corners of his mouth tipped up. "On one hand that makes me happy. On the other hand, I'm dying."

Viv wasn't the most sexually active woman and pregnancy wasn't an option with her history. But now was definitely not the time to start verbally going through her medical chart.

"I'm clean," she told him. "And you don't have to worry about pregnancy."

His eyes turned darker as he lowered his lids once again. Before she could question him, he slid his mouth across hers and murmured, "I'm clean, too."

Viv tightened her grip around his waist, urging him to take what they both were so desperate for.

The second he joined their bodies, he locked his eyes on hers. This was what she'd been waiting for. This man, this moment.

Viv arched into him, her fingers gripping his

shoulders as he set the pace. Jack captured her mouth, nipping at her lips over and over as his hips met hers. He reached down, curling his hand around the back of her knee and lifting just enough for her to feel even more sensations rushing through her.

Viv tore her mouth from his the second her body started to climb. She squeezed her eyes shut, not wanting him to see just how affected she was by the intensity of their passion.

Jack's lips on the side of her neck, drifting down to her sensitive breast, was all she needed to peak. Her body clenched around him as she cried out. He jerked against her, his own body stilling as he followed her into oblivion.

Moments later, Viv continued to tremble. Jack kissed her once more, then rested his forehead against hers. His heart beat harshly against her chest and she wanted desperately to know what he was thinking. Then again, the silence of the moment was perfect. She could relish the fact that she'd made love with the one man she'd wanted for years. He'd come to her because he'd been unable to fight the attraction any longer.

Could he just walk away after this? Could he be satisfied with just one night and then go on as if this didn't alter their lives?

Viv turned her head aside as guilt and fear trickled through the euphoric state she'd been floating in.

The journal was behind her closet door. The key to Jack's past was only feet away. She'd been looking for the right time to talk to him, but this certainly wasn't it.

"You were right earlier," he murmured against the side of her neck. He rolled slightly so his weight wasn't directly on her, but he kept an arm around her waist. "I was scared when you called. It's not an emotion I connect with or have often."

Viv jerked her thoughts from the journal and shifted to face him.

"My wife died when I was overseas, and I wasn't there to protect her." He held Viv's gaze as his thumb stroked her abdomen. "She was in the wrong place at the wrong time. I know I may not have been with her even if I had been stateside, but knowing I was so far…"

Viv slid her palm over his stubbled cheek. "You don't have to explain why you were afraid. I know your wife died while you were overseas. I didn't know specifics, though. You aren't to blame. You have come to grips with that, right?"

Jack eased away and rose to his feet, instantly leaving her chilled. When he started gathering his clothes, Viv knew he was holding true to his word. What just happened was all he would give. There would be no opening up and sharing past stories now.

And how could she expect him to reveal a part of himself, when she held such a damning secret?

"I'll be on the sofa."

His parting words left her cold. She wished he

would have just gone home, because what had taken place in her bed hadn't drawn them closer together at all. If anything, she felt more distanced than ever.

# Ten

Jack glared across the coffee shop, willing Ryker Barrett to step through the etched glass doors. After last night, Jack wasn't in a great mood, which was perfect for a meeting with the man who knew all the O'Sheas' secrets.

Sipping his black coffee, Jack tried to ignore the ache in his chest. Last night had been everything he'd wanted, everything he hadn't known he'd been missing. But there was no way anything could ever come from hooking up with Viv. She was all about taking care of children, and he refused to allow himself the luxury of even entertaining the idea of a family life.

He'd had sex. He certainly wasn't looking for holy matrimony. Once was enough. The risk of going through such heartache again wasn't something he

was on board with. Besides, no permanent relationship could come from an affair with his assistant,
even if he were looking for something long term.

Which was why he'd found himself hightailing
it from her apartment before she and Katie woke.
He'd gone back to his Beacon Hill home to change,
dodged all questions from Tilly and had made it out
to Bean House, hopefully in time to catch Ryker.

Jack had done enough surveillance to know the
man frequented this coffee shop next to the O'Shea
offices. He wasn't surprised that Ryker had picked
this neutral territory for their meeting.

Jack waited nearly twenty minutes before he spotted the man in the dark leather jacket, with coal-
black hair and a menacing look in his eyes. Ryker
Barrett was exactly what he portrayed: mysterious
and standoffish, and exuding a go-to-hell attitude.

Well, too bad. Jack was eager to get this little
powwow started.

After Ryker placed his order, Jack stepped to the
end of the counter and met the man's gaze, relieved
not to see recognition there.

"Get your coffee and meet me over in the corner."

He didn't wait for Ryker to answer. Even though
Jack had been at the O'Sheas' Christmas party, he
hadn't spoken to Ryker that night, so it was unlikely
the family's right-hand man would link him to Viv.

Just as Jack took a seat, Ryker came to stand on
the other side of the table. Coffee cup in hand, he
glared down at him.

"You can sit or stand, but you may not want everyone to hear our conversation." Jack wasn't in the mood for games.

Ryker sipped his coffee, then slid the wooden chair out and casually dropped into it. He glanced around the café as if he didn't have a care in the world. Arrogant jerk. Jack wanted to reach across the table and punch the smug look off his face.

"I've already told you everything, which is more than you deserve." Ryker flung an arm across the chair beside him and set his cup on the table. "You have two minutes."

Jack knew if he wanted to get to the bottom of this case once and for all, he'd have to take a different approach. "I'm willing to work with you to find out who committed the crime against the Parkers," he said grudgingly.

There was a ring of truth to the saying about keeping your enemies closer, even if Jack hated every second of it.

"And why would I want to work with you?" Ryker countered.

Jack shrugged, leaning forward on his elbows. "Because you want to clear the O'Shea name and I want to find out who made an orphan out of an innocent child."

Even though Jack had a gut feeling he was looking at the main suspect. But if he could work closely with Ryker, and Viv kept digging at the office, there was no way they could miss the truth.

"You've been hell-bent on pinning this on us," Ryker stated. "Why the change now?"

"I'm determined to get to the truth. You can either work with me or get out of my way."

Ryker's dark eyes narrowed. "Threatening me isn't your smartest move."

Jack couldn't help but smile. "That wasn't a threat. That was a promise."

Determined to keep the upper hand, Jack pushed himself to his feet. "Talk it over with your friends and let me know."

Gripping his to-go paper cup, Jack headed out the café door and into the brisk February air. There wasn't a doubt in his mind he'd be contacted by Ryker or another member of the O'Shea clan in short order. If they were truly going legit in the legal sense—and Jack wasn't so sure about that—then they'd want to work to clear their name and get the Feds off their backs.

Jack sipped his hot coffee as he made his way to his SUV. He'd head into the office, because he wasn't in the mood to go home and face Tilly. After he'd spent the night at Viv's apartment, there was no way Tilly wouldn't know something was up. She'd caught him sneaking in this morning and he'd dodged her questions, but he couldn't forever.

First, he had to come to grips with what had happened last night before he could even attempt to make excuses to his nosy, yet loving, chef and maid.

Logically, he knew he shouldn't have slept with Viv, but there was no way he could've avoided her forever. The more he worked with her, the more he wanted her. The physical aspect he could deal with, and thoroughly enjoy. It was everything else that came after the sex that had him questioning what the hell he was doing.

Like why he was still thinking of her. Thinking of the way her hair had spilled around him, the way she'd looked at him with hope, as if their one night could lead to something more.

Jack climbed in behind the wheel of his SUV and brought the engine to life. He'd been up front with Viv, telling her that he was unable to give more, and she'd agreed. But her face as he'd dressed and left the room said differently.

They both needed time apart. Unfortunately, that wasn't possible, since they were working so closely together. Jack had to keep the upper hand on his emotions or he'd find himself falling deeper for Viv. And that was a heartache he couldn't afford to revisit.

He'd avoided her for two days.

Viv sat behind her antique mahogany desk and willed her door to open. She'd come in and gone straight to her own office like she did every morning she was scheduled to work with Jack. But this morning was unlike any other. This was her first day back to work after sleeping with her boss.

The phrase sounded so clichéd and tacky, but there was no sugarcoating the truth. He'd left her bed before she'd fully recovered, and spent the night on the sofa, then slipped out before she was up for the day. Clearly, he meant what he'd said about one night being all he could give.

Viv would be lying if she didn't admit she'd hoped he'd change his mind. Did he feel anything at all toward her? Was a one-night stand all he wanted? The man was so closed off, she honestly had no clue.

In his defense, he hadn't lied to her.

Viv dropped her face into her hands as guilt consumed her. Jack may have had sex with her and left, but at least he'd been totally up-front with her. As opposed to Viv, who was still hiding a secret that would completely change his life and everything he thought to be true.

The timing hadn't been right, then their attraction had snowballed and they'd slept together. Now here she sat, half in love with her boss and trying to help him bring down the family that was his by birthright.

From this point on, nothing would be easy. Not her feelings, not her actions…absolutely nothing.

Viv jumped when her cell rang. Glancing to the ID on the screen, she quickly slid her finger across to answer.

"Hello."

As if her heart wasn't already beating fast enough, now she waited to see what the social worker wanted. If it was time to say goodbye to Katie, then she'd have to let the precious baby go. But Viv wasn't ready.

"Vivianna, I hope this is a good time."

"Of course." It wasn't like she was actually working. "What can I do for you?"

"I'm calling with a question that I'd like you to take your time to consider."

Viv eased back in her leather chair and crossed

her legs. "All right." Smoothing her pencil skirt down her thigh, she gripped her cell in anticipation.

"Before you took Katie in, you had expressed interest in full adoption. Is that still an avenue you'd like to explore, or are you content with fostering? I'd like to make it clear that Katie has no other family members."

Hope blossomed in Viv's chest. Being a parent had been a dream she never thought she'd reach. She'd put her forms in to adopt because she did want a family. She'd thought someday she'd be okay with erasing that distance between her and the foster children she helped, but honestly hadn't known if that day would ever come. Was Katie the one to be part of her family?

To know she could fully adopt a baby so sweet, so perfect... Viv was almost afraid to get too excited.

"Adopting is definitely an option," she replied, unable to hide her smile. "But I have questions and concerns."

"Of course. I'm happy to answer anything. Would you like to take some time to think, to fully process what this means? There are so many things to consider. Cost, time, paperwork. You're a fostering veteran, so you've already gone through a great deal of the process."

Viv came to her feet just as her office door opened. Of course Jack would decide to barge in now. She held up a finger and he nodded as he sauntered over and took a seat in the leather club chair across from her desk.

Viv turned her back to him and concentrated on the view out the window. Snow swirled around, piling on top of the three inches that had already been dumped on Saturday.

"I'm definitely interested in talking with you further," Viv stated, well aware that Jack was likely hanging on her every word. "Why don't I call you in a day or two? Maybe by then I'll have my questions all made out and we can go over everything at once."

"Perfect. And Vivianna, there's no pressure here. We can find a home for Katie. I just thought you would be the best candidate for her."

Viv blinked as tears burned her eyes. "Thank you. I'll be in touch."

She disconnected the call and held on to her phone as she crossed her arms. Adopting Katie would be a dream come true. The little girl she'd come to love and care for could possibly be hers forever. Her heart swelled nearly to bursting.

"Viv?"

Jack's voice pulled her from her daydream. Composing herself, she turned to face him, thankful the desk still sat between them as a barrier. She could handle only so much at once.

"Everything all right?" His eyes held hers and he frowned. "You're crying."

Viv swiped at the stray tear that had escaped. "Everything is fine. What did you need?"

"First I need to know why that call has you upset."

Viv leaned over her desk chair and placed her

phone back on her calendar. "Nothing that has to do with work."

Slowly, he pushed himself to his feet, never taking his eyes off her. "Is this how things are going to be?"

"You mean a professional relationship?" she asked, crossing her arms. "Isn't that exactly what you decided on? I'm just following orders like a good assistant."

Jack rounded the desk, those green eyes never wavering from hers. He came to stand toe to toe with her, forcing her to tip her head back. Viv didn't step away, but nerves spiraled through her.

"Don't make things difficult," he growled. "When I see you upset, I have to know why."

"And you have no right to ask." Oh, how she wanted to share this news with him, but after he'd all but sprinted from her bed, she just couldn't expose herself to any more hurt and rejection. "My personal life has nothing to do with you. Now, I'll ask again. What did you barge in here for?"

The muscles in his jaw ticked. "I spoke with Ryker on Saturday. I offered to work with him in order to solve this case."

Now Viv did step back, mostly from shock. "What? What did he say?"

Shoving his hands in the pockets of his Italian suit, Jack shrugged. "We battled back and forth. I left before he could turn me down, but I'm sure he'll think about it. He'll discuss the offer with Braden and Mac, and with Mac coming into town, one of them will reach out to me."

"You think they'll agree to work with you?"

"I have no idea, but I'm not giving up and I had to find a new tack."

Viv closed her eyes. If he knew about the journal, perhaps he could approach them in a different way. Maybe they'd be more willing to speak if they knew Jack was family.

But first and foremost, Jack was an investigator and security specialist. He was still the enemy, according to the O'Sheas. So for now, the journal and the secrets would remain locked safely in her closet.

"I'm going in early tomorrow to talk to the Feds," Viv told him. "I know everyone will be at the office."

"There's nothing to be nervous about." Jack reached for her, then dropped his hand before he could make contact. "They haven't discovered anything to incriminate you."

Oh, but *she* had. Something much more life-altering than clues that might solve a mysterious case.

"I told you about the files I copied," she countered. "That was months ago and I haven't taken anything else, but the O'Sheas are convinced someone on the inside is betraying them."

"The Feds won't ask you anything that will be damning in front of Braden or Mac."

Jack did reach for her now. His hands curled around her shoulders and she couldn't help but stiffen at his touch.

"I don't want you worried. I'll take care of you."

Viv laughed. "Right. For the case, I know." She shrugged away from his touch. "I have work to do."

Jack fisted his hands at his sides. "And ignoring the other night is part of that?"

Oh, that was rich coming from him. "Says the man who couldn't get out of my bed and dressed fast enough."

# Eleven

There was no way to avoid this conversation, but Jack just wished like hell he didn't have to see that hurt in her eyes. How was he protecting her when he was the one causing her pain and frustration? He should've kept his damn hands to himself. But the slippery slope he'd been clinging to for months had become too much.

"Don't do this."

"What?" she asked, tilting her chin in defiance. "Call you out on the truth?"

"Damn it, Viv." Jack raked his fingers through his hair. Propping his hands on his hips, he forced his eyes to stay on hers. "You're everything I used to want."

Great, now he'd exposed a portion of himself. Letting anyone see that side of his heart wasn't an option, but the words hovered in the air between them and he wished like hell he could snatch them back.

Viv's brows dipped as she frowned. "I don't even know what that means."

He'd come this far. Viv deserved the truth after the way he'd blurted out half of it.

"As you know, my wife died while I was overseas."

He hated thinking about that time in his life, let alone talking about it. Yet somehow he felt the need to open up to Viv about it for the second time.

Other than Tilly, Viv had been in his life the longest since his darkest hour. If anyone deserved to be let in, it was her. Besides, he prided himself on being truthful whenever possible.

Viv had always been an open book, never pushing for more in return. Her loyalty, her honesty and her commitment to stand by him even during his moody days were humbling…and that was the only reason he was opening up to her. It had nothing to do with the fact he'd felt a connection while he'd been in her bed. That connection couldn't go any deeper and she would understand why soon enough.

"My wife was shopping when a robber decided to randomly open fire. He turned the gun on himself before the cops arrived."

Jack swallowed, turning away when moisture gathered in Viv's expressive brown eyes.

"She was shopping for baby furniture," he whispered, when his own emotions threatened to take hold.

Viv's audible intake of breath pulled his focus back to her. "I wasn't there with her. I only had one month left in the service and I was getting out, because we were planning the family we always wanted."

"Jack."

Viv reached for him…and he let her. Perhaps he needed the contact, or maybe he was just a glutton for punishment, because he wanted more of her touch whether it was the right thing to do or not.

She took his hands, squeezing them in hers as she stared up at him. "I don't even know what to say."

Tears spilled down her cheeks. He'd never had someone shed a tear for him before, never let anyone get close enough to care.

"I know that pain," she whispered. "Losing what you want more than anything in this world."

He opened his mouth to question her, because there was definitely a story there, but she kept going as if she hadn't just alluded to a dark past of her own.

"But you're the strongest person I've ever known. Don't you want to move on and take back what was stolen from you?"

Jack gritted his teeth. "I want to bring down criminals who skirt the law and believe they're above reproach."

She let his hands drop as she reached up to frame his face. "And what about your personal life?"

When she stared at him in such a caring way, Jack realized that, their passionate night of sex aside, she got him. She understood him because she had her own demons.

"I opened myself up once, Viv." He gripped her wrists and eased them away from his face. "I won't make that mistake again. I've chosen to devote my life to seeking justice."

"Even at the cost of your own happiness?"

Jack let go and stepped back. "I have homes in three countries, so much work I'm turning clients away and I'm about to bring down the biggest Mafia family Boston has ever seen. How could I not be happy?"

The corners of Viv's mouth tipped in a sad smile. "The fact you equate happiness with material things tells me all I need to know."

She pulled her office chair out and took a seat. Jiggling the mouse on her computer, she brought her screen to life. "I have some emails to sort through. Go ahead and close the door on your way out."

Jack stared at the back of her head for a split second before he whirled her chair back around. Leaning down, he curled his fingers around the arms. Her eyes widened in shock as he jerked the chair even closer, so their faces were only a breath apart.

"I warned you once about dismissing me," he murmured against her mouth. "Just because I refuse to commit doesn't mean I don't still crave you."

He crushed his mouth to hers, damning himself for letting his emotions guide his actions. Reaching up to grip his hair, she didn't hesitate in opening for him.

Encircling Viv's waist with his hands, Jack hauled her up against him. Without breaking contact, he shifted until he was leaning against the edge of her desk and she stood between his legs.

One taste wouldn't be enough. He'd known that the moment he'd stepped into her bedroom. He was doomed to repeat the performance, and he didn't give a damn if they did it right here in her office.

A chime interrupted erotic thoughts of Viv spread out on her desk, begging. He wanted to ignore the cell in his pocket, but business always came first.

Viv tore her mouth from his, taking a step back and smoothing her skirt down. Shoving her hair behind her ears, she turned to face the window, as if she were ashamed.

He'd have to deal with that later. He'd wanted a kiss, and damn it, he wasn't going to deny himself anymore when she wanted it, too. Jack pulled the cell from his pocket and answered without looking at the screen.

"Jack Carson."

"Jack, Braden O'Shea. I hear you're looking to work together."

In an instant, Jack's back straightened. "Braden."

Viv jerked around, eyes wide. Jack had to ignore the swollen lips he'd just tasted. His body was still revved up from having her plastered against him. Her curves were something he couldn't deny himself... and that was going to have to be addressed sooner rather than later.

"I'll meet with you on my terms," Braden stated.

"Depends on the terms," Jack retorted. He wasn't about to hand over control so easily.

"You can come by our main office on Friday after we close. We're a bit busy this week."

*Yeah, with the Feds breathing down your neck.*

"Friday it is," Jack agreed. "See you then."

"One more thing."

Jack gripped the phone, pinning Viv with his gaze as he listened. "What's that?"

"If you try to play both sides, you'll regret it."

Jack laughed. "Threats don't work on me. You'd do best to remember that."

He disconnected the call, making sure Braden knew full well going into this little meeting who was in charge.

"He threatened you?" Viv whispered.

Jack slid the cell back into his pocket and waved a hand. "We came to an understanding."

Viv wrapped her arms around her abdomen. "If you get hurt…"

"I'm fine. This all will come to an end soon."

Pursing her lips, Viv glanced down at the floor. She was a confident woman, one of the qualities he found so damn sexy, but something was wrong.

"About earlier—"

She jerked her eyes back up to his. "Don't apologize."

"Fair enough, since I wasn't going to." He reached out, palming her face with his hand. He stroked her full bottom lip. "I want you in my bed. *My* bed. I won't make excuses or promises. You're what I crave and I intend to have you again."

She swiped the tip of her tongue across her lip, catching the pad of his thumb and sending another jolt of arousal through him.

"Maybe I want more than just to be the one to scratch your itch."

Jack laughed as he hauled her against his body once again. "Honey, you're not just scratching an itch. I've had that before."

"So what am I?" she pressed.

"You need a label? Can't this just be simple?"

Viv laughed in turn. "No, it can't."

Jack pulled in a deep breath, careful to choose his next words wisely. "I can't name this, Viv. What we have… I've never done this before. You're my assistant, my friend."

"Your lover."

He nodded. "That's what I'm offering, no more."

She cocked her head with a quirk of her brow. "Is everything a business deal with you?"

"There's no other way to live."

Viv stared back, silence heavy in the narrow gap between them. "There's every other way to live. Happiness, building on your dreams, raising a family."

And all that had been robbed from him, making him detach from ever wanting such luxuries again.

"Looks like I only scratched that itch, after all," she murmured. "I have goals I'm moving toward and I won't let anyone get in my way…no matter how much I may care for him."

Viv turned away and circled her desk as she headed out of her office. That jasmine scent clung all around him, mocking him with the promise of a woman he'd had, but never would again. And he had nobody to blame but himself.

# Twelve

Viv sank into the desk chair in her office at O'Shea's. After an hour of answering questions from the Feds, with Braden, Mac, Ryker and Laney all present, her nerves were shot and she needed a moment to herself.

She was still reeling from the emotional roller coaster she was on with Jack. One minute he was telling her no, the next he was kissing her as if he needed her more than air. She wanted him, that was never in question. But she'd also come to realize she deserved more than an occasional romp whenever *he* wanted…which was exactly the tacky proposal he'd delivered.

Katie's adoption was another emotional standoff Viv found herself in. Her first instinct was to say absolutely yes, but that was the selfish side of her. She wanted to truly think about this from every angle. Viv had lain awake most of the night worrying if she could provide the best environment for Katie to grow up in.

She lived in an apartment, with no yard for a child to play. She was a single parent, and Katie deserved two.

But Katie was comfortable with her. They were already a team in the short time they'd been together. Letting Katie go to another family would be crushing, not just for Viv, but possibly for the baby, too. Even though she was just shy of a year old, Katie had already experienced enough trauma in her life. Stability was essential for children.

Approaching footsteps had Viv snapping out of her reverie. Braden.

"You have a second?"

As if she'd tell him no. Viv nodded and came to her feet.

"Sit down." He motioned with his hand as he crossed to the accent chair across from her desk. "I appreciate you coming in early and going over the Feds' questions with me. They have a tendency to be redundant, trying to get us to slip up."

"I have nothing to hide." Lie of the century. "So there's no slipping up."

He gave a clipped nod as he crossed his ankle over his knee. "Loyalty is of the utmost importance in our line of work. We appreciate you hanging in there through this past year. It's been a bit of a rocky road."

Viv offered a smile, despite her stomach clenching

in knots. "I need the job and I value family. Working here is a perfect fit for my lifestyle."

Braden laced his fingers over his abdomen and held her in place with those intense green eyes of his. "How is the foster situation going with Katie?"

As tightly as her lies were woven, she always had to prepare a quick response in her head before she delivered it. One misplaced word or action could be detrimental to not only her, but Jack, as well. Despite whatever was going on with them personally, she would never jeopardize his work.

Viv let out a sigh. No way was she going to reveal the fact she might be adopting Katie, either.

"It's going really well. Katie has adjusted and I'm planning a little cake and a fun outing for her birthday next week. If the weather cooperates we'll go sledding."

"Bring her out to the estate. We have plenty of room and slopes."

Viv stilled, hoping her smile didn't falter. She'd been to Braden's home only once, for the Christmas party where Jack had insisted on being her date, albeit in disguise.

If she was invited to their house again, clearly they continued to trust her and didn't suspect a thing. Yet Viv couldn't help but wonder if any of them even knew that journal existed. Most likely not. She'd found it shoved in the secret compartment in the top of her desk…a desk they'd assigned her to.

Unless it had been a plant. Would she be pulled into some downward spiral by failing a test?

Paranoia was not her best quality, yet she couldn't help but look at this scenario from every possible angle. That's the only way she could be prepared for the fallout.

"I may take you up on that," she replied. "I know she's only turning one, but I want her first birthday to be special."

"She's lucky to have you." Braden eased forward in his seat, planting his elbows on his knees. "I'd like to ask you something."

Why did she have to be so on edge? He was just a man. A powerful, mysterious man who might or might not be on his way to prison.

"What's that?"

"Would you consider coming on here full-time?"

Shocked, she shifted in her seat. Definitely not what she thought he was going to ask. Not that she had a clue as to what he'd been thinking, but never once did she consider they'd want her here more often.

"I know you have Katie to think about, as well, but we'd be more than happy to accommodate you if you need to bring her in every now and then." Braden's chiseled face broke out into a wide smile, softening his harsh features. "It's not like this place won't be filled with babies soon enough, anyway."

With his own wife and sister expecting, Braden was definitely immersed in the baby world. This was one area he was going to get a crash course in very shortly.

"How soon do you need my answer?" She'd have

to discuss this with Jack, and see if it was even possible for Martha to watch Katie more often.

"Laney would like to start working from home more, so you'd be picking up a little of her work, plus Zara and I would be coming in to take up the slack, as well. If you could just let me know in the next few weeks."

Hopefully, in that time the case would be wrapped up and she wouldn't be here. Part of her couldn't help the guilt that settled heavily in her chest. Over the past year, she'd gotten to know the O'Sheas. No matter the rumors surrounding them, or how Jack felt about them, she truly believed they wanted to move forward and just focus on auctions and growing their family. They might obtain some of their items through less than legal ways, but they weren't hardened criminals. Or murderers.

Patrick O'Shea may have done things differently, but Viv would bet just about anything that Braden, Mac and Ryker had nothing to do with the Parkers' deaths. Still, there was no evidence either way.

"I'll think about it," she assured him. "Katie is my top priority right now, so I need to do what's best for her."

Braden came to his feet. "I wouldn't expect any less from you. I'll let you get back to work. We have the final inventory list coming in this morning. I believe there are seventy-two pieces for you to input."

Viv nodded with a smile. "I'll be looking for the email."

Once she was alone, she blew out a breath and

rubbed her temples. If she were a drinking woman, she'd take a whole bottle of something strong right about now. But she was a simple girl, and a scented bubble bath and a good book would do the trick... Too bad she had no time for the mental breakdown she deserved.

And at the heart of everything going on was Jack. He'd gotten her into this impossible situation with the O'Sheas, he'd turned her emotional life inside out and he'd left her wanting more. She'd walk through fire for that frustrating man and he was willing to settle for a romp in the sack.

Some fantasies weren't meant to be fulfilled. She just wished she could get the image of him in her bed out of her mind. Each time she lay down, she felt him, ached for him. And she didn't know if she'd ever get over that need.

Tilly had the week off, but she'd come by and prepared food to keep him going and promised to leave him alone. She was either worried he'd starve or she was nosy...and he knew the answer.

She'd given him a wink and told him she'd made more cheesecake. Damn it, the woman knew his plans for the night and he hadn't even said a word. Which was why their relationship was utterly perfect.

Still, she could make all the cheesecakes she wanted, could throw him that knowing grin and think she knew what he was up to during his personal time, but she had no idea.

In all honesty, he couldn't grasp his own thoughts

lately, not when it came to Viv and all the unwanted emotions she'd conjured up.

Tonight, though, he'd called her to his house because of business. No other reason. He wouldn't even let his mind go down the path toward anything personal. He'd offered her all he had to give; she'd turned him away. They wanted completely opposite things in life, which he'd known going in. But that didn't stop him from wanting her.

Jack downed the rest of his whiskey just as his doorbell rang. He slammed his tumbler onto his desk and headed down the curved staircase. The exterior lights shone on Viv, revealing her shape through the etched-glass door. There was no mistaking that luscious figure. His hands itched to touch her intimately. Hell, he'd been aching for her since he'd left her bed days ago.

As soon as he used his fingerprint on the security panel and opened the door, he knew the possibility of having her tonight wasn't on the table. Not that Katie on her hip was the issue, because she'd fall asleep eventually, but Viv's eyes narrowed on his a half second before she pushed her way into his foyer.

"Good evening to you, too," he muttered as he closed the door.

"You demand I come by after work and won't tell me why." She slid the hood off Katie's head and Jack reached over and eased the baby from Viv's arms. "So I rushed to pick her up and get here, thinking something was wrong, but as I'm driving in this hellacious weather, I realize nothing is wrong and you're just being you."

Jack unfastened Katie's coat as Viv jerked her own off and flung it over the banister. She took Katie back, then removed her coat and tossed it there, as well.

"So, now that we're here, what could you possibly want that you couldn't text or call about?"

Jack crossed his arms and didn't even try to hide the smile that spread across his face. Was now a bad time to tell her how damn hot she looked when she got worked up? Because this fire and passion shooting from her was seriously turning him on.

Damn it. He didn't need to be more turned on by her. He needed to cool it. She wanted things he'd given up on. And she deserved every bit of what she worked for. He just wished she'd give in to what they both wanted while she was on the path to her dreams.

"What's the smirk for?" she asked, her eyes narrowing even more.

"I've never seen you so…"

"What? Frazzled? Losing my sanity? Confused and terrified all at the same time?"

Jack closed the space between them, instantly regretting that he hadn't taken better care to protect her. She was fine physically, but he should've seen that this entire process would take its toll on her emotionally. Not to mention the fact that she was a single mother. She gave to everyone but herself, always and in all ways.

"Something happen?" he asked, searching her

eyes for the hint of tears. If she shed any, he'd be a goner. He could handle anything but the vulnerability of a woman, especially this woman. The instant tears came onto the scene, he was ready to slay any proverbial dragons on her behalf, even if that meant himself. And he'd hurt her, he knew that, but he was trying like hell to never do it again.

"Just the Feds in today, questioning me again."

"I listened to the audio. You did amazing."

He'd been so damn proud of her for sounding so confident, giving the same answers she'd given time and time again. But with the Feds still working the case, things would look suspicious if Viv wasn't questioned just as much as the rest of the staff and family at O'Shea's. He and Viv had gone over her story and background so much before she'd ever started working for them, there was no way she would flub up. He'd made sure she was mentally armed before going into enemy territory to do his battle.

And that still pissed him off. He hated placing her inside, knowing she was getting tangled up in that corrupt family. The sooner he could bring them down, the better off they'd all be. At this point, he was itching for them to screw up and just get a parking ticket—anything to open up the field to investigate every aspect of their lives.

Katie struggled in Viv's arms and Viv eased her down onto the floor. Jack watched as the infant pulled herself up, holding on to Viv's legs. She gripped the hem of Viv's pencil skirt and started glancing around the unfamiliar territory.

Yeah, his house wasn't kid friendly.

"So what was so important?"

He focused back on the woman before him, the woman he shouldn't want, but did, almost as much as he wanted to solve this case.

"You're moving in here with me."

# Thirteen

Viv laughed, sure she'd heard him wrong. "Nice try. What do you really want and where is our chaperone?"

Jack rested his hand on the newel post and leveled his stare at her. "Tilly is on vacation for the next several days and you are moving in. It's not up for debate."

Who the hell did he think he was?

"I don't know what plan you have in that overactive mind of yours, but I can't move in here." She pointed down to Katie, who had started crawling around the hardwood floor of the foyer. "We're a team."

"Move her in, too," Jack stated, as if things were that simple.

Viv shook her head and crossed her arms. "What

has gotten into you? I turn down your oh-so-romantic proposal of sleeping with you at your beck and call, so now you're trying to overcompensate by having us live together?"

"Damn it, no." He blew out a breath and rubbed his hand over the back of his neck. "I think you'd be safer here. If Braden were to piece things together or get a hint that we're working together… It's just too risky. You've already heard suspicious noises at your apartment. Next time I may be too late to help."

Viv nodded, fully in agreement about the safety issues. "I can work from home for you, so why jump to the conclusion that I'd be safer here?"

"First of all, the security in your building is ridiculous."

Viv rolled her eyes and crossed to the entryway to the formal living room. Katie was off exploring and Viv knew from experience that she needed to keep her eyes on the active child.

"You have to have a code to enter my building. I'm perfectly safe. I'm sure a neighbor was moving furniture or something and I just overreacted."

When Katie started crawling toward the stone fireplace, Viv intervened. The last thing she needed was the baby climbing up onto the hearth and falling. As if sensing the end to her fun, Katie turned and speed-crawled toward the low coffee table. Thankfully, there was just a variety of classic novels on display and nothing breakable.

When Viv turned toward the wide, arched doorway, Jack met her gaze. Leaning against the frame, he had his arms crossed and that look on his face that said he wasn't in the mood to argue. *Welcome to the club.* She wasn't too keen on having been summoned here to have this insane conversation.

"If there was nothing else, we'll head back home. I've never been a fan of driving in this crazy weather."

Didn't matter that she'd lived here for years, she still didn't like navigating the narrow Boston streets when they were snow covered.

"We need to talk, so if you want to go home tonight, I can drive you, or I can take you home in the morning."

Viv glanced at Katie as she pulled herself up with the help of the coffee table. Maybe Viv could lower her blood pressure if she counted backward from one hundred. She doubted it, and she didn't have the time. Jack seemed to be under the impression that she would just do anything he commanded.

"You should know me well enough to understand I don't do demands." Viv circled the table and took a seat on the leather sofa. The thing looked like nobody had ever sat there, which was probably true, considering Jack wasn't the most social of butterflies. "I'm safe where I am, but I will agree to not go into your office until this is all over. That's the compromise."

Jack pushed off the door frame and stalked toward her, his eyes never wavering. When he stood only inches from her, Viv smiled.

"Intimidation may work on your adversaries, but I'm not afraid of you."

Turned on, reliving every moment of their night together in vivid detail, but not afraid.

"I won't let you get hurt. And if Braden figures all of this out…"

Jack's growl sent shivers through her. Knowing what she did about his past, about the crippling loss he'd suffered, was the only reason she wasn't grabbing Katie and leaving. He was scared…for her. How could she be angry about that?

Still, she wouldn't be bullied into staying here. For her own sanity, she couldn't. She was half in love with him, and being under the same roof, faux playing house, was not an option.

"I'm not going to get hurt," she informed him. "Actually, I was offered a full-time position at O'Shea's."

"When was this?"

"Today." Viv peered over her shoulder just in time to see Katie heading back to the fireplace. "Braden came in and talked to me after the Feds left."

Katie protested when Viv picked her up. Jack's house was definitely a bachelor pad. Yet another reason they wouldn't be staying here.

"And what did you tell him?"

Viv pulled off her bangle and handed it to Katie. Promptly, the gold bracelet went into the infant's mouth, but at least she wouldn't choke on it. Jewelry, the new teething ring for on-the-go mommies.

"I said I'd think about it and get back to him."

Exhaustion set in and Viv went back to the un-used sofa and sank down. She slid her shoes off, not because she was staying, but because there was only so long she could be "on." She'd reached her limit for the day.

"I explained that I needed to think about what was best for Katie, but I knew I needed to talk to you, as well."

Jack came to sit next to her. Resting his elbows on his knees, he leaned forward and stared across the room. "I don't like this," he murmured.

Confused, Viv shifted in her seat, tucking Katie into the crook of her arm. "I thought you'd jump on board. Having me there every day would give us the leverage we need."

"I think they know something."

Viv shook her head. "I don't agree."

Jack's dark brows rose. "And why is that? Because you've become so chummy with them?"

The hurt in his tone made her feel guilty. She certainly had plenty to feel guilty about, but not because she'd gotten to know the notorious family on a personal level. She wanted justice for whoever killed Katie's parents, but didn't happen to think it was her fake employer.

"I don't want to argue with you."

Viv started to rise when Jack placed his hand on her knee.

"Stay."

The simple command had her stilling beneath his touch. Jack had a way of looking at her that made her want to obey his every word, and that irritated her. She couldn't let herself get swept into his world.

He didn't want her there on a personal level and she had a damning secret that would blow everything out of the water.

Inevitably, the situation would come to a head, and she knew for a fact they'd both be hurt in the end. "I'll take the full-time position," she told him. "It's the smart move. I can work from home in the evenings for you, plus I'll be alone some if I'm a regular employee there. This will bring us closer to solving the case, I know it."

Jack blew out a sigh and shook his head. "I don't like it, Viv. If you find something incriminating, you can't take it. They may not suspect you yet, but this is a test. If anything at all happens, you'll be to blame."

Katie wiggled down once again, taking Viv's bangle with her. "I'm aware of that. I won't do anything to raise a red flag."

Viv knew where all the security cameras were, knew nearly all the passwords to various accounts and she'd be the contact people would speak to if she was the only one there.

The irony in all this? She'd been completely innocent in her actions when she'd stumbled upon Patrick's journal. When she actually tried to snoop, she'd discovered very little. She'd copied those files in the hopes something would be in them, but no such luck.

Which only went to confirm her own suspicions about the O'Sheas being exactly who they claimed to be.

"I want to know your every move, every contact, even what you eat for lunch."

Viv laughed. "Don't you think that's a bit much?"

He leveled his gaze at her. "Where your safety is concerned? It's not enough."

Shivers slid through her at his throaty tone. That whole dominating, protective trait was the sexiest part about him…and he had a whole lot of sexy going on. There was no way she could be this close, inhaling his masculine scent, and not recall exactly how he felt with his weight pressed against her. The way his hands had traveled over her body was a memory she'd carry forever. Even though he hadn't stayed in her bed, their intimacy was one of the best moments of her life.

She needed to leave. Unless they were strictly discussing business, she needed to keep her distance, because she only wanted him more, and she had no right to.

Every part of her wanted to tell him about that journal, but trumping her need to be truthful was the guilt she felt about being the one to hurt him. And knowing who his father was would destroy him. His passion for justice would come second to the cold, hard truth of his paternity.

Jack jumped up from the sofa and sprinted across the room. Viv came to her feet in time to see him grab Katie before she could climb onto the stone hearth.

Great. She'd been fantasizing about her boss and totally ignored Katie's safety. If that wasn't a sign she needed to get her priorities straight, she didn't know what was.

"Nice try, speedy." Jack scooped Katie up and did some mock airplane moves around the room. Frozen in place, Viv could only take in the sight. He would've been a great father. His protective side was obvious, but this playful side was something she hadn't seen. Jack would've put his family first, above all else. He might be a big shot in the industry and moving into global territory of security and investigating, but the smile on his face right now told her everything she needed to know.

The man wanted a family. He didn't want to be as closed off and hard as he came across. She'd witnessed his caring nature time and time again. And watching him right now had Viv's heart tumbling in her chest. Jack would be the perfect husband, father. He'd be the fiercest protector and greatest provider.

There was no denying the fact, now that she'd fallen face-first in love with Jack Carson. She'd tried to dodge her deeper emotions, hoping she was just physically infatuated. But no. She admired everything about him, and at this point, being with him would never be an option.

Tears pricked her eyes. Blinking them away didn't help as they slid down her cheeks. She swiped at the dampness with the back of her hand and pushed her hair behind her shoulders.

As Jack spun around, he zeroed in on her and stilled. Pulling Katie close to his chest, he strode over to Viv.

"She's fine," he assured her.

Viv nodded, emotions too thick in her throat to form words.

"What is it?" he pressed, patting Katie's back.

His large hand covered Katie's entire pink floral jumper. Such a strong man who'd had so much taken from him, and Viv was only adding to his heartache… only he had no idea.

Another round of tears hit and she didn't even try to hide them. She needed to tell him the truth. Viv loved him and he deserved to know. In the face of her feelings, this case was nothing.

Jack's free arm wrapped around her shoulders as he pulled her to his side. Viv instantly rested her head on his shoulder, even though she had no right to. Seeking comfort from the man she was lying to was hypocritical, at best.

"Jack, I—"

Katie reached out and fisted a handful of Viv's hair.

"No, no." Jack twisted his body, pulling Viv slightly to the side. "She's a grabber. Apparently, everything goes into her mouth."

Viv squeezed her eyes shut. The words weren't coming. She'd just fully confessed to herself that she loved him, and here she was, ready to tell him a secret that would destroy him. Why did life have to be so complicated?

"What were you saying?" he asked.

"I'm sorry," Viv sniffed in an attempt to compose herself. "I guess I'm just tired from work and trying to figure out what to do for Katie's party."

"I'll help plan the party. Tell me what to do."

Viv laughed, the room blurring before her from the moisture in her eyes. "You plan first-birthday parties often?"

Jack glanced down at her, his crooked smile melting her heart. "Never, but how hard can it be? She's one. She has no expectations yet."

"I know." Viv moved from his hold, because it was so easy to lean on him, to draw from his power and strength. "I just want her to have the best."

"She will. I'll make sure of it." Jack glanced at Katie, who was toying with the tiny button holding down the collar of his dress shirt. "Right, speedy? You'll have the biggest cake and a roomful of presents—"

"Let's not get carried away," Viv interrupted. "My apartment isn't that big."

She smoothed her silk blouse back in place and dabbed beneath her eyes, sure her mascara had run against her splotchy skin. If there was ever an Ugly Crier award, she'd win hands down.

Of course, if she weren't waging such an epic internal battle, then there wouldn't be an issue.

"Stay here tonight," Jack told her, looking back her way. "You're exhausted."

Viv shook her head. "I'm fine. Besides, there's only a few diapers left in my bag and Katie doesn't have the stuffed animal she hugs when she falls asleep."

The intensity of his gaze warmed her. The man inside who had loved and lost was still there. Would he ever make a full appearance? Would he ever let down that guard again and open himself up to a relationship?

She hurt for him. She hurt for the life he'd been through and the truth he'd yet to discover. She loved this man, wanted more than anything to be with him, but she couldn't form the words.

"Don't look at me like that, Viv."

"I see the truth," she whispered. "I know you want more and you just won't let yourself feel."

His jaw clenched. "I can't afford to feel. Not anymore."

"Then I'll be living in my own apartment and working from there." Viv reached for Katie, who protested and reached back for Jack. "We're going home, sweetie."

Turning from Jack and those mesmerizing eyes, Viv made her way to the foyer. He fell in step behind her, but she ignored him as she busied herself getting her and Katie's coats on.

"I want to know when you're home."

Viv picked Katie up, securing her on her hip. "You don't have that luxury, considering I'm only your assistant."

She circled around him and jerked the door open. "I'll see you in the office—actually, I won't, because I'll be working from home—"

Jack's hand flattened on the door, slamming it shut and closing out the cold air. She whirled around, but before she could say a word, he kissed her hard and fast before he released her.

"You're more than my assistant, so quit throwing

that in my face," he commanded. "You will tell me when you reach home because I care. Damn it, Viv. I care too much and that's the problem."

When he said things like that he made it damn near impossible to stay angry.

Reaching behind her, she turned the knob. "It's only a problem for one of us."

# Fourteen

Four days had passed without any real contact from Viv. Without hearing her laugh, her soft tone of voice. Without seeing those expressive eyes as she watched him when she thought he wasn't looking.

Four. Days.

Evidently, Viv was holding her ground and not having anything to do with him if it didn't involve work. She'd been only emailing or texting. He hadn't even heard her voice over the phone. Fine. He could handle this switch.

But he didn't like it. He hated every moment that had passed without her. Damn it, he missed her.

He'd noticed a void by the end of day one. A hole in his life that only Viv filled. When had she become so important, so permanent in his life, that he was miserable without her?

The office was boring as hell and it smelled…not like her jasmine scent. Her cheery yellow-and-white office mocked him every time he passed by. He finally closed the door on the second day.

But having her work from home was the smart move to make. Wasn't it? He wanted her safe, out of harm's way as much as was possible with this messed-up case.

Now, after four days of not seeing her face, Jack stood at her apartment door with an insane amount of shopping bags—he'd left the boxes in his car. Katie's birthday was today and Viv had texted him that she was doing a cake and maybe taking her sledding in the park. There was no way in hell Jack was going to ignore that invitation.

Because not only had he missed Viv, he'd missed Katie. He wasn't quite sure when he'd become attached to the innocent girl, but he couldn't wait to wish her a happy birthday.

As he gripped the bags, he wondered if he'd done too much. What was the protocol for buying presents when a child was in temporary housing after being orphaned? In Jack's opinion, there was no maximum amount…as he'd just proved with his no-limit credit card.

The neighbor's door opened and Jack groaned inwardly, pasting a smile on his face as he turned to see Martha poke her head out.

"Oh, nice to see you again," she said with a wide smile. Her eyes darted to the bags in his hands. "Are those for Katie? That is one spoiled little girl."

He wasn't about to mention the dollhouse or the motorized convertible toddler car he'd left in his SUV.

"You only turn one once, right?"

Viv's door opened, saving him from further conversation with the nosy babysitter.

"Jack. Come on in." Viv peeked out the door and waved to Martha. "Thanks again for the stuffed elephant. She loves it. I'll bring you some cake in a bit."

Her neighbor winked. "Take your time."

Ushering Viv back in, Jack threw Martha a nod and followed her. Once they were inside, Viv closed the door with a giggle.

When she laughed her beauty was like nothing he'd ever seen. She was absolutely breathtaking. With her hair down around her shoulders, a simple cream sweater hugging her every curve, Viv was the quintessential girl next door, but she was as complex as any woman he'd ever known.

And he wanted her. The attempt to get her to move in with him was legit; he was worried about her safety. But he wanted her under his roof where he could keep his eyes—and his hands—on her.

Damn it. He shouldn't want this. Yet there was no way he could stop the ache, the need.

"I've never seen anyone scare you." She continued laughing. "Yet you're afraid of my elderly neighbor."

Jack didn't reply. There was no denying the truth. That woman terrified him.

He glanced around the open apartment. A bundle of pink balloons lay on the small dinette table, while white and pink streamers were twisted around every stationary object. Two cakes sat on the kitchen counter, a small one with a large purple *1* in the middle and a larger one that was pink with white-and-purple polka dots.

"You've been busy," he commented, setting the bags down.

Her eyes darted to the load he'd carried in. "I hope all of that is not for Katie."

"I actually have more in the car," he told her, feeling like a fool when her eyes widened. Perhaps he had gone too far, but whatever. He wasn't sorry and he still believed Katie deserved everything and more. "I had a problem choosing just one item."

"Jack." Viv closed her eyes and sighed before meeting his gaze again. "Go get the rest."

Stunned, Jack tilted his head, narrowing his eyes at her. "You're not angry?"

"Does it matter?" she laughed.

"Not really. Once I got to the store and the clerk started showing me all the new things that had arrived, I just kept adding to my pile. Honestly, if I'd had more room in my car, I would've bought more."

Viv's hand went to her forehead and she began rubbing her temples. "I don't know why I'm surprised, but…okay. Just go get the stuff and I'll get Katie into her birthday outfit."

Jack darted out the door and made quick trips, grateful not to get caught by Martha again. He was nearly out of breath by the time he'd carried everything into Viv's apartment. Obviously, he needed to

up his workout routine. He'd been a little preoccupied lately to get in all the miles and lifting he was
used to.

As he closed the door the final time, he realized his
purchases had pretty much overtaken her apartment.
Wrapped boxes in various colors, with thick bows,
littered the living area; the bags he'd brought in first
circled the dining table. Between all the variegated
shades of pink, there was no denying this was a little
girl's birthday party.

Katie came crawling out of the bedroom wearing
a polka-dot top with some ruffles around the hem.
She seemed to match the theme of the newly decorated apartment. He may have gone overboard mon-
etarily, but Viv had seriously thought this out and
wanted something special for the little girl.

Viv stood over Katie, reached down and took her
hands. Suddenly, Katie was on her feet, wobbling
toward Jack.

His heart swelled. How could he be so excited
to see her learning to walk? He wasn't invested in
her...was he?

No. Absolutely not. She wasn't staying with Viv.
One day, probably soon, Katie would move on to the
family that would give her a forever home.

Still, he couldn't help but smile. He wasn't completely detached from emotions.

"When did she start this?" he asked.

Before he realized his actions, Jack found himself
squatting down and reaching for Katie. That wide,
two-toothed smile tugged at strings he thought had

been severed years ago. This sweet child didn't have a care in the world. How could he not smile back? How could he even think of anything going on in the outside world when she was teetering toward him, those bright blue eyes locked on his?

"She started a week or so ago, but she's getting stronger."

Viv let one of Katie's hands go and Jack took hold. Together they walked toward the dining area. The image of a family hit him hard and he attempted to tamp it down, but damn it, this was everything he'd wanted. A woman like Viv was exactly what he'd be looking for if he wanted a family. She was perfect in the way she cared for Katie, the way she was sexy and sweet, the way her cheeks flushed when he caught her looking at him. She'd called him first when she'd been scared, so she trusted him to protect her. At one time that's all it would've taken for him to get her and keep her in his bed, his life.

But that man was gone. His dreams had been murdered. There would never be a future with Viv. His sexy assistant would have to remain just that. And working with her day in and day out was wearing on him.

Somewhere along the way, though, his wants had changed, and they looked too much like everything Viv was offering.

Was it even possible to have that life he'd once wanted? After ten years of grieving, of burying himself in work and building his empire, could he actually put a personal life back in place?

Katie let out a squeal. "Up, up, up."

Jack didn't hesitate and didn't even question who Katie was requesting pick her up. He merely reached down and swung her into his arms. The weight of her little body, the slender arm that rested behind his neck... There was something so special, so perfect about her.

And maybe he could slowly ease back into the idea of having his own family one day. He knew his wife would've wanted him to move on.

"I've never done this before," Viv stated. "Should we just let her dive in to her cake first?"

Jack laughed. "I don't think there's a rule here."

Pulling out one of the chairs, he took a seat and situated Katie on his lap. "Bring her cake over and let's see what she does."

Viv's eyes widened. "She's going to get you filthy. Put her in her high chair."

Jack shrugged. "We'll be fine. I have other dress shirts."

He maneuvered his arms around Katie so he could fold up his sleeves while Viv went to get the cake. She placed one white candle in the top and set the confection in front of Katie.

"Hold her arms back while I light this."

Viv pulled out a lighter and lit the candle. With a smile, she pulled her cell from the pocket of her jeans and held it up. "Should we sing?" she asked.

"Sure."

Jack started "Happy Birthday" and didn't feel silly at all, sitting in a sea of pink. If anything, he felt…hopeful. Damn it. He deserved to have this. He *wanted* to have this.

While Viv sang and snapped pictures with her phone, Jack motioned for Katie to blow out the flame. Of course she had no clue what was going on. Jack met Viv's eyes, the smile on her face making something inside his heart clench. Before he could assess the emotion, she leaned toward the candle. Together, they blew it out.

Jack reached out and slid his finger along the icing. He showed the glob to Katie, then took one of her hands and guided it toward the cake.

And that was all he needed to do. She dived in to the white cake and colorful icing with both hands, bringing fistfuls of the clumpy mess to her mouth. She rubbed her hair, rubbed his pants, turned and smeared some across his lips.

Viv laughed, still snapping pictures.

Jack licked his lips. "This is really good. You made this?"

"I did. I'm not much of a baker, but I figured I could handle a simple cake recipe."

Viv set her phone down and went to get napkins— pink-and-white polka-dot ones, of course.

"About the other day—"

She shook her head, cutting him off. "I don't want to discuss it. Forget about it."

Surprised at her flippant response, Jack eased the cake closer to Katie before meeting Viv's intense stare. "Isn't that supposed to be my line? I wanted to forget everything, but I can't."

"For now, let's focus on Katie." She smiled, warming him in places he thought would always be cold, empty. "And discuss where you think I can possibly keep all the toys you bought."

He didn't want to discuss toys. He wanted to discuss how he'd ached for her since he'd last seen her. He wanted to discuss how he'd handled the situation poorly.

But mostly he wanted to discuss how they could erase this sexual tension between them, which was more prominent than ever. And he had a feeling there was only one way.

# Fifteen

Jack discarded his dress shirt straight into the trash. It wasn't even worth having Tilly take it to the cleaners at this point. The icing appeared to be permanently embedded, which was just fine. He honestly didn't recall when he'd had a better time…at least not in the past ten years.

His dress pants weren't faring much better, but he couldn't exactly walk around in his black boxer briefs and light gray T-shirt. He'd scrubbed out as much of the pink icing as he could, but only managed to grind it in more. Tilly would scold him, but whatever. His tailor in Italy wouldn't mind making a new suit.

Viv had taken a sugar-loaded one-year-old back to the bath. Poor Katie could barely keep her eyes open, but her ringlets had been dripping icing and she needed a good scrubbing.

While he was alone, Jack attempted to tidy up, but he was wondering if he should just buy Viv a new condo. It would take days to get her tiny apartment looking like it once did. Granted, with all the purchases he'd made, the living area would look like the toy department at Saks as long as Katie lived here.

Unwelcome emotions suddenly clogged his throat. He'd gotten attached to the innocent child, when he'd told himself he wouldn't. But only a heartless person could look in that sweet baby's face and not feel a connection. She demanded affection and damn if he didn't want to give her everything. Toys were one thing, but he wanted her to have the perfect family. That would mean leaving…which would destroy Viv. Hell, he was beginning to think it might destroy him, too.

He'd give Viv the world and her every desire if he were in a better place. She deserved to have everything handed to her. More than anything, he wanted to be that man who could do that. But he couldn't risk the pain to his already battered heart.

Attempting to focus on things he could actually control, Jack took a trash bag and started gathering up the wrapping paper and empty boxes. Once that was done, he piled the toys on one side of the living room. When he turned back to the dining area and kitchen, he groaned inwardly. There was no way that was going to come clean without something akin to a pressure washer.

When Viv stepped into the living area, she glanced around and let out a laugh. "We survived."

Jack took in her disheveled hair, ends damp from the bath and a glob of icing dangling on one side. She'd stripped off her sweater and now wore a simple white tank that hugged her breasts and dipped in at her waist. As messy as her appearance was, Jack wanted his hands on her. Now that he knew the way her silken skin felt beneath his palms, his need for her was all-consuming.

But after this family moment they'd just shared, seducing her wouldn't be the wisest decision. Everything from this day was temporary: Katie, Viv, Jack, the party, the appearance of domestic bliss.

"Why don't you go shower and I'll figure something out in the kitchen."

Shaking her head, Viv crossed to the chaos on the table. "I'll clean this up. You didn't come over to get assaulted by a birthday cake. You can head home."

She threw him a glance over her shoulder. "Where's your shirt?"

"Trash."

Her eyes widened. "I can wash it for you. There's no need to just throw away a good shirt."

He shrugged. "I have more at home."

Viv rolled her eyes and focused on gathering everything inside the plastic tablecloth she'd laid out. "I'm not going to offer to wash your pants."

Jack couldn't hold back the smile. "If you want me to take them off, just ask."

Flirting was dangerous, but he could control himself. He'd help her clean up and then be on his way. It was getting late, but where else did he have to be? Nobody was at home, and for the first time in years, he didn't want to go back to that empty place where his own breathing echoed in the halls.

"Keep your pants on and help clean if you insist on staying," she said with a laugh. "Just grab a garbage bag and hold it open."

Jack pulled another bag from the roll beneath her sink and shook it out, holding it in front of her. When she turned with the bundled tablecloth and pieces of mashed cake, she tripped, sending the whole gooey mess onto his chest.

Her eyes immediately went to his. "I'm so sorry," she gasped.

Jack dropped the sack on the hardwood floor, scooped up a hefty amount of icing with his hand and flung it. The glob landed just at the scoop of her tank, disappearing into her cleavage.

Her eyes narrowed, but the glimmer of mischief there warned him this war had just begun. He quickly picked up the discarded bag and held it out as a shield, but not before she scooped up another chunk of hot-pink icing and smashed it into the side of his head.

As he reached down for more discarded cake, Viv ran toward the living area, her hands stretched out in front of her. "Okay. Truce."

The wide smile, the brightness in her eyes... Even smeared with cake—especially smeared with cake— she looked sexy as hell.

"I don't think so," he stated, stalking toward her. "You got me twice. I owe you one."

"Jack, it's in my shirt," she argued, taking another step back until she hit the side of the sofa. "We're even. I didn't intend the first attack—I tripped."

He jerked one hand out to grab her arm, pulling her against him, then smeared the icing over her chest with the other. Slowly, he stroked that exposed skin just above her tank, keeping his eyes locked on hers. Viv shuddered beneath his touch.

"You're not...playing fair," she murmured.

Jack snaked his arm around her waist. Trailing his fingers up to her mouth, he spread the last of the icing across her lips.

"I'm not playing at all, Viv."

Tipping his head down, Jack held her close as he slid the tip of his tongue over the icing just below her collarbone. Her breath hitched, so he did it again.

"Jack."

The way she whispered his name set off a fire inside him he didn't know existed. Gripping her hips, Jack aligned her body perfectly with his.

"You drive me crazy," he muttered against her lips. "I tried to ignore you, ignore this. Damn it, Viv, I want you."

Her fingers threaded through his hair, urging him closer, and it was all he could do to not rip her clothes off and take her to the floor.

"Then have me."

She covered his lips with hers, demanding he turn his words into actions. No problem. He slid his hand inside the back of her tank, palming her bare skin. Her body arched against his as she tore her mouth away and started licking the icing off his jawline, his neck. His body was strung so tight, but he didn't want just a quickie.

"I want more than just your bed tonight," he told her.

Viv lifted her head and smiled. "Then maybe we should start with a shower, where I can thoroughly clean you."

Every part of Jack's body tightened as he lifted her off her feet and headed toward the hallway. Viv wrapped her legs around his waist.

"Go to the bathroom in my bedroom," she whispered in his ear. "My shower is huge."

Anticipation gnawed at him as he turned the corner to her room. The second he set her on her feet, he grabbed the hem of her tank and yanked it over her head. Icing and cake crumbs covered her lacy white bra. Jack wasted no time in bending down to lick every last bit, until she gripped his shoulders and trembled beneath him.

Reaching behind her, he flicked the closure of her bra until it sprang free. She flung it aside.

Jack fisted his T-shirt and slid it over his head, sending it to the floor. Her eyes raked his chest before she reached for his pants. Jack glanced down, watching as she continued to undress him. Those delicate hands shook as she eased the zipper down.

He toed off his shoes and kicked away his pants.

"I want you in that shower now," he growled. "So

if you don't want to go in with your pants on, I suggest you take them off."

Her eyes widened as she quickly went to work, and within seconds she was gloriously naked before him. Jack reached for her, seizing her by her waist. He backed her into the bathroom, keeping his eyes on hers.

"I've never had a food fight before," he told her. "I better be thorough with the cleanup."

Viv reached between them, covering him with a gentle stroke of her hand. "I like a man who's thorough."

Mercy, she was going to be the death of him. There was nothing sexier than a woman who took charge and knew what she wanted.

The corner shower had two glass walls and a rain head. Jack opened the door and reached in to turn the water on, testing the temperature before stepping in and pulling her with him. He positioned her directly beneath the spray, smoothing her hair away from her face.

Droplets dotted her skin. Jack's hands roamed up and down her sides, needing to feel every bit of her.

"Tell me what you want," she murmured.

He spun her around until her back hit the tiled wall. "Every inch of you."

Sliding his hand between her legs, he stroked her. Viv's head tipped back, her eyes lowered. Every time he touched her, she shook with need—a need he completely understood.

Her hips pumped against his hand and Jack

couldn't take his eyes off her. There was nothing more erotic than a woman about to come undone at his touch...*this* woman. She was different than any other, an epiphany he'd come to so recently, he was still reeling from the shock to his system.

Viv panted as she turned her head to the side, squeezing her eyes shut. Water trickled over her flushed skin, catching on her lips a second before she slid her tongue out to wipe it away.

The moment her body tightened, Jack captured those lips. He hadn't been kidding when he'd said he wanted every single inch of her. He swallowed her groan as she gripped his biceps. Having her cling to him was everything right now.

When she finally stilled and pulled away, she blinked against the water and met his gaze. When she bit that swollen bottom lip, Jack removed his hand and reached up to frame her face.

"Whatever you're thinking, leave it." He kissed her fast, hard. "It's just us here. Nothing else matters."

Wasn't that what she'd been trying to get him to see? She'd been urging him to live again, to find happiness again. Part of him, a part he'd just revived, desperately wanted to risk his sanity for that happiness. He wanted to know what taking a chance on a relationship would do.

Tears filled her eyes. "I need to—"

He nipped at her lips. "I need *you*. Nothing else right now."

Her brows drew in as she studied him. Her hesitation had worry spearing deep inside him. "Are you having second thoughts?" he asked.

"No." She shook her head and reached up to grip his wrists. "No. I'm just…nothing. I want this, I want you. Are you sure? Because the way you left the other day…"

"Right now, right here, this is all that matters." He couldn't express his feelings, was still struggling to come to grips with them himself. "I need you, Viv."

Admitting that was a leap for him. He never needed anyone, ever. But Viv was his. She had been for a while and he was finally realizing just how much he ached for her…and not just physically.

Her arms circled his neck and her ankle locked behind his knee. "Then take me."

Jack lifted her against the wall, pinning her in place with his body. She wrapped her legs around his waist and began to rock her hips against his.

Staring at him from beneath thick, dark lashes dotted with water, she whispered, "Make me yours again."

How could he deny the lady?

Jack gripped her hips and joined their bodies. With no barrier between them, he stilled, taking just a second to bask in everything Vivianna. She was utterly perfect and she was completely his.

With an arch of her back and a moan, Viv urged him to move. She closed her eyes and bit down on her lip as he complied, but he was having no part of that. If she was going to be his, then she was going to damn well know it.

"Look at me," he commanded.

Her dark eyes locked on to his. Jack kept one hand firmly on her hip and gripped her jaw with the other before crushing his mouth onto hers. He craved more. She was like a drug and he couldn't get enough. Would he ever?

Her knees dug into his waist as Viv pressed even closer. The warm spray beat all around them and Jack knew he'd never take another shower without imagining her thrusting her body against his with total abandon.

Viv's body quickened and she gripped his shoulders. He eased back, needing to see her come undone again.

She held his gaze as her body tightened around him, thrusting him into his own release. He didn't look away, couldn't if he wanted to  Viv's expressive eyes most likely mirrored his own. So many unspoken emotions…

Jack clenched his teeth, fighting the urge to say something. Any confessions stemming from feelings during sex were not smart. Later, when they were lying in bed, he'd say what he needed to, what she deserved to hear.

When her body went lax, Jack rested his forehead against hers as he came down from his own release.

"Jack—"

He kissed her. Whatever she was about to say would have to wait. Right now, he was reeling from the fact he was falling for a woman, the first in over a decade. And he had no idea how the hell that would fit into the life he'd created…a life he'd intended to live alone.

# Sixteen

He'd wrapped her in a thick bath towel and carefully laid her in bed before climbing in beside her—as if this was part of their daily routine.

Viv blinked back the tears, thankful for the darkness. His feelings for her had changed. Somewhere along the way, he'd started falling for her. She'd seen it in his eyes, tasted it on his lips and felt it with every single touch.

There was so much he didn't know, so much he deserved to know. She had to stop being such a coward and just tell him, reveal the most damning secret. But the words wouldn't come. Viv lay in the crook of his arm, her hand resting directly over his heart. "I can't have children," she whispered into the darkness.

As if that was the only secret she'd been keeping from him. Nerves spiraled through her as the inevitable conversation hung in the air. But this was at least one truth she didn't mind sharing. The reality of never having her own children had caused an open wound so deep inside her, she hadn't revealed it to anyone. She wanted to with Jack. She wanted to share everything…but the lie that she'd held on to for weeks would likely be the hurdle they could never jump together.

"Have you tried?" he asked. He stroked her shoulder with his thumb, sending a shiver through her.

Viv pulled in a shaky breath. "I'm infertile. I was sick when I was younger. The choice was never mine."

He squeezed her tighter against his side, turning to kiss her forehead. "That's why you foster."

Wrapping her arm around his waist, Viv nodded. "I don't have to give up my yearning for children, and I can help many. Fostering is the best fit for me. I'm single, so it would be more difficult to raise a child on my own."

As she explained her reasoning, the heaviest weight she'd ever known crushed her chest.

"You're an amazing woman, Viv."

She didn't want his praise, and she sure as hell didn't deserve it.

"I'm actually thinking of adopting Katie. I was asked and I… I think I'm going to move ahead with the process."

The idea both thrilled and terrified her. She was

so excited to be a mother, and sweet Katie was an angel. But could she do it on her own? At least with fostering she had gaps between children, could decide when she was ready to open her home again. She could keep her heart from getting involved—though with Katie she was already a goner. But adoption was permanent and Viv wanted to make sure Katie was getting the best life possible. Would one parent be enough?

Jack shifted to lie on his side, facing her. "I can't think of anything better for you or her. She's lucky to have you."

"I want to give her everything," Viv confessed. "I just don't want to make a mistake."

Jack's soft laugh filled the room. "You wouldn't make a mistake. When you come into anyone's life, they're better for it. Katie... Me..."

Viv's heart clenched. "Jack—"

"I need to tell you that you mean more than—" He broke off with a muttered curse before continuing on. "Damn it, I want this, Viv. I want to see where this will go, how we can make this work. I can't promise anything. Hell, this is all still new to me, but I know when I'm not with you—"

"Stop."

She couldn't listen to his declaration. Once he knew everything, every last part that she had to share, then he could decide...and Viv knew in her gut that he wouldn't feel the same. Still, she had to tell him. This wasn't about the case anymore, this was about family. If they were going to have any

chance at being a couple, a family with Katie, he
needed the truth now.

In the glow from the baby monitor, she found it
hard to look at him. But she couldn't wait another
minute. The dynamics in their relationship had
shifted immensely and as much as she wanted to
wait for the right time, she knew in her heart such a
moment didn't exist.

It was now or never.

"I—I've learned something about the case," she
whispered, tears threatening to clog her throat.

Jack propped his head on his hand and stared
down at her. "When? Today?"

"A few weeks ago." She closed her eyes. "I didn't
know how to tell you."

"Weeks?" he repeated. "What don't you know
how to tell me? Damn it, Viv, I need to know everything. Don't worry about how to break news to me."

Silence settled between them and already the wall
separating them was being erected. She'd been building it brick by brick the second she'd opted to keep
that journal hidden.

"How the hell could anything you discover be up-
setting to me?" he went on. "What could you possibly have learned?"

Viv never wanted to be the one to destroy Jack.
His need for justice overrode everything in his life.
She knew he had to have all the facts. But even now,
on the brink of blowing this case, she couldn't tell
him.

She rolled over, flicked on the lamp and headed to

her closet. Without a word, she reached up to the top shelf and pulled down the leather journal. She'd read it front to back, twice. She knew the secrets Patrick O'Shea had kept, knew more than just Jack being his son. She'd read about how his children wanted him to go in a more legal direction, but he'd been hanging on to contacts he couldn't cut ties with.

Turning back around, she met Jack's gaze. Those green eyes pierced her from across the room. He glanced at the book she held.

She'd never been more vulnerable in her entire life. Viv stood before Jack wearing absolutely nothing... except the truth clutched in her hands. Completely bared to him, Viv willed herself to push through this, to do the right thing.

With her arm extended, she walked to his side of the bed and handed it to him. Jack kept his eyes on her as he took the journal.

Finally, he shifted his focus to the leather-bound book in his lap. He opened the cover, immediately seeing Patrick O'Shea's name.

Jack jerked his attention back to her. "You've had this for how long?"

Viv swallowed against the guilt, the remorse. There was no going back now. "Too long," she whispered.

Unable to look at his face, coward that she was, Viv grabbed her robe from atop the comforter and jerked it on before heading to the antique trunk at the end of her bed. She took a seat, facing away from Jack. Twisting her hands in her lap, she imagined each word he was reading. She knew where the bombshell was located within the pages; he had a few more to go.

Each time he turned another, Viv cringed.

Jack's audible gasp gutted her. Still, she couldn't face him.

"You read this."

His accusing tone was like a slap. "Yes."

"And you didn't think I deserved to know this bastard was my father?"

Viv came to her feet, tightened the belt on her robe and turned to face him. The pages lay open, Patrick's dark penmanship mocking her.

"Of course you needed to know," she said, knowing she had no right to feel wounded. "I wanted to tell you the second I found it. But I—"

"What?" he demanded as he jerked the sheet aside and came to his feet. He reached for his boxer briefs from the floor and tugged them on. "You got too close with the family and shifted your loyalties?"

Stunned he'd even think that, Viv shook her head. "No. Never. I never shifted my loyalties to them. I may believe in my heart they're innocent, but I am on your side, Jack."

His laugh mocked her. "Really? I'd hate to see if you were my enemy. How the hell do I even know this journal is real? It could've been a plant. Did you ever think of that?"

Viv nodded. "I've thought of this from every perspective. But I wasn't snooping when I found it. The one time I was actually just doing my job, I stumbled upon it."

In a rush, she explained how it was caught in her desk, but the way it was wedged in, she truly didn't believe it had been placed there to trick her.

"Conveniently, it was *your* desk," he replied in that dry, disbelieving tone. "So why now? You waited until we'd grown closer for what? Because you thought it would soften the blow somehow?"

"No," she whispered. "I just… I couldn't keep it from you any longer. I'm falling for you and—"

"Don't say it," he demanded. When he started gathering the rest of his clothes, Viv's heart sank. He wasn't even going to stick around to hear her defense… not that she hadn't seen this coming. "Don't even try to tell me that you love me, or any other feelings you're having. At this point, what you want, what you feel, is irrelevant."

He stepped into his pants, shrugged his T-shirt on, then grabbed the journal. "You know how much this case means to me. You're the only person I've confided every damn thing to. I've confessed my fears to you because I knew you understood from being on the inside."

The disappointment in his tone was worse than the rage. He'd trusted her. He'd placed her on this particular case because he knew she'd always been loyal and honest.

She'd failed him.

"I can't take back what I did," she explained, crossing her arms over her chest. "I was scared when

I first found it, worried I was being set up to see what I'd do with it. But as I read on, I figured there was no way the O'Sheas knew you were their half sibling. Braden would've confronted you. So then I tried to find the right time to tell you."

"The second you found it was the time," Jack countered, narrowing his eyes at her. Only moments ago those eyes had held her in place with passion and signs of love. "But you clearly chose the team you're on. And it's not mine."

Katie's cry blared through the monitor. Viv jumped from the unexpected intrusion, then glanced at the screen. Katie turned, grabbed her favorite blanket and quieted down.

Jack sat on the edge of the bed to pull on his socks and shoes. "Everything you've learned, from the journal and otherwise, needs to stay with you until this case is wrapped up. Clearly, you'll need to stay at O'Shea's, because the Feds are counting on you, but I no longer need you to do work for me."

He didn't look at her as he delivered the toneless speech. Cutting her out of his life was that quick, that final. As much as she wished he'd listen to her reasoning, she knew Jack wasn't that man. He saw things as black-and-white, and his once-glossy perception of her had been tainted. Quite possibly, his need for justice had been tarnished, as well. How could he take down the only family he had left?

As much as it hurt to let him walk away angry, she truly had no choice. He needed to think, and she needed to let him go. She loved him, more than she thought possible. But for now, she'd keep things professional—and live with the gaping hole he'd left in her heart.

She hoped in time he'd come around, hoped he'd realize that she loved him and had done everything to protect him.

"Do you want me to stay on with the O'Sheas full-time?" she asked.

Jack's mocking laugh rang out as he rose to his feet. "I'll text you the name and phone number of the contact from the FBI. You can direct all of your questions to him from here on out. I'll have your things from your office sent over."

With the leather journal in hand, he headed toward the bedroom door. He stilled at the threshold and threw a heartbreaking look over his shoulder.

"This isn't how I planned the night to end." His eyes held her in place from across the room. "And to think I nearly let my guard down and told you how I truly felt."

By the time she processed exactly what that veiled statement meant, he was gone.

Viv clutched the V in her robe as she sank to her knees. Tears gathered and fell as she struggled with the reality that Jack had fallen for her. He didn't need to say those exact words; he'd shown her.

Swiping at her eyes, she glanced at the monitor. Sweet Katie slept peacefully now. Viv had done the right thing in finally telling him. It didn't matter what her heart wanted, all that mattered now was that child and giving her the best life.

But that didn't mean Viv would let go of what she'd found with Jack without a fight.

Sometimes seeking comfort is the only way to get through the mourning process. I had no idea a child would come from our intimacy. As much as I want to be part of his life, I respect Catherine Carson's wishes. I came into her life, offering nothing, so the least I can do is stand by her in a silent manner and support her from a distance.

It kills me. Goes against everything I stand for. I take what I want, what's mine. And this little boy with green eyes like my own is mine.

Sending checks isn't the same, but he will want for nothing.

Jack stared at the words, hating every single one of them. At this point he even questioned his loyalty to his own mother. She'd lied to him by remaining silent. She'd never once hinted that his father was the notorious Patrick O'Shea, but here it was, in plain sight.

Easing back in his leather office chair, Jack stared at the open pages, willing them to rewrite history. He didn't want to be the son of such a criminal. He'd done nothing these past ten years but take down jerks like him.

Yet here he sat, at a crossroads, and he had no idea how the hell to move forward. What direction did he take at this point? Did he confess to the Feds that he was too close to the case now? Did he go to Braden, Mac and Laney and tell them…

What? What would he say? "Congratulations, it's a boy"? Somehow that didn't sound right: There was no "right" way to go about this, yet Jack had to make a decision and he needed to make it fast.

He swiped a hand over his face, instantly smelling something floral. Jasmine. The shower he'd taken with Viv had left its mark on him. There was no escaping her.

The idea that she'd had this information for weeks tore him up. He'd lost sleep over the case, had gone to the enemy, had quizzed her over and over. Yet she had remained silent.

He'd slid right into her world, trying like hell to remain closed off, but where Viv was concerned, he hadn't had a choice. Everything about her drew him in, from the way she took in foster children to the way she called him out when he was being difficult.

She had curves that any man would beg to touch, and he'd done so much more. He literally craved her, ached for her. How did he just turn that off?

And sweet Katie had gotten into his heart, too. How could he ignore that emotion? An innocent baby had stolen his heart when he wasn't looking.

But Viv made him smile, made him want… Made him realize there was enough life left in him to do exactly what he'd intended, and that was to have a family of his own.

She'd helped him in a sense, but in the end, she'd

destroyed him. If she cared for him the way she claimed, she would have come to him first.

Falling for Viv wasn't what hurt. Knowing she didn't trust him with the truth cut him so deeply, he didn't know if he'd ever recover from the wound.

But there was only one thing he could do at this point. The Feds didn't need to know about Jack's biological connection to the O'Sheas—at least Viv was right in that area. They only wanted Jack's help with proving or disproving the theory that the family had something to do with the Parkers' deaths.

Uncovering the truth about his past, his family, was more important to Jack than any damn case.

For once in his life, something was coming before work.

When he glanced at the antique clock on the corner of his desk, he realized time had literally slipped away from him. It was nearly six in the morning. He'd left Viv's house so late, then come straight to his home office and bottle of twenty-year-old bourbon. He'd read Patrick's damn journal cover to cover, trying to make sense of it all.

Jack had no doubt this book was legit, and he highly doubted the rest of the O'Sheas—*his siblings*—knew anything about their father's deepest secrets.

Tapping the edge of his desk, he continued to glare at the black ink. He'd wait a bit longer before making the call. A call that could change his entire future.

Jack tipped back the rest of the bourbon in his

tumbler. His thoughts drifted to Viv again, and he damned himself for ever letting her into his life.

He cursed himself further for still wanting the hell out of her.

But that was something he'd have to address later...after he met with his newfound brother.

# Seventeen

Neutral ground was always his first choice, but for this little meeting, Jack had agreed to go to O'Shea's. Mac was still in town and Jack wanted to meet him and Braden together. He wanted to go through this story only one time, though he knew that wasn't likely.

Jack entered the offices an hour before they officially opened. He'd been up all night and called promptly at seven. Braden had agreed to the emergency meeting, though Jack could tell the tycoon wasn't too thrilled with the demand. Too damn bad. Jack's life had spiraled into a cursed mess in the past twelve hours and he was done getting smacked in the face by fate.

He figured the only way to get them all together

was to tell them he had information about their father. Which was the truth.

Clad in a black dress shirt and black pants, Braden stepped out of the back. Jack couldn't stop the punch to the gut as he stared into the man's green eyes. The same shade he saw every morning in the mirror. How had he never noticed the resemblance?

Because there had been no reason to until now.

"This better be good, Carson." Braden motioned for him to follow. "Come on back. Mac is here and Laney will be along shortly."

And where Laney was, Ryker was. Arrogant prick.

Jack clutched the journal in his hand and headed toward the back. He expected to feel a little fear, if he were being honest with himself, but right now all he wanted to do was get this over with. The odds of losing control were in his favor, after all, this meeting was going to be four against one. But he'd gone against odds before. Jack never backed away from a challenge. Besides, he held the journal—of which he'd made copies—and he also had more ties with law enforcement than the O'Sheas could ever hope to have.

Jack stepped through the doorway to the back office and met Mac's angry stare. With a clipped nod in greeting, Jack surveyed the rest of the space. He hadn't been in this part of O'Shea's before. He knew from Viv's description that the mahogany desk in the corner was hers.

Bringing Viv into his thoughts right now would

not help him get through this meeting. He needed to focus 100 percent on what was about to happen, because this journal didn't affect just his life—he was getting ready to drop a bomb directly onto the people he'd despised for so long.

Ruining them had to take a backseat to the truth. He wanted them to know exactly what he'd discovered.

And after reading Patrick's words, Jack had a gut feeling he might be trying to bring down the wrong individuals. His father—it still hurt to think of Patrick O'Shea in those terms—had been the one who'd needed to be brought to justice for his past crimes. Braden, Mac and Laney were all guilty by association, but they'd pleaded their innocence in this case all along. Ryker...well, he brooded and threatened, but he'd maintained his story, as well. Perhaps Viv had been right all along. Maybe this family was innocent and were only hypothetically guilty because of their notorious name.

"What couldn't wait?" Braden asked as he took a seat behind the oversize desk in the middle of the room. "It must be something big for you to agree to come here."

The journal felt heavy in his hand. "I've stumbled upon some information."

And he'd thought hard about how to admit where it came from. He might be feeling hurt and betrayed by Viv, but he wasn't about to out her in front of this family. Even he wasn't that big of a jerk.

"There's no easy way to do this," he admitted

as he crossed into the room and laid the journal at Braden's fingertips. "This was your father's."

Mac, who'd been silently leaning against the desk, glanced down to the leather book. "How did you get this?" he asked, turning his focus back to Jack.

"That's not important. What's important is what is inside." Jack swallowed, but he kept his features taut. "Halfway in, you'll see a date flagged—June 30."

Braden blew out a sigh, as if he'd rather be anywhere else than talking with Jack barely after sunrise. Well, Jack would rather be anywhere else, as well, but there was no escaping the inevitable.

Keeping his eyes on Braden, Jack propped his hands on his hips and waited. Moments later, the man slid the open pages to his brother.

"Where the hell did you get this?" Braden demanded. "I suppose you believe you're the son?"

Jack nodded. "I know I am. Catherine Carson was my mother. Patrick refers to her often, and my mother never told me who my father was. I know we were taken care of, because when I turned eighteen, I received a lump sum of money. There's no way it came from my mother, who worked in a flower shop."

Mac held the journal in his hand and gestured with it. "So because you find this out of the blue, and the time line adds up, you just assume—"

Jack held out his palms. "I'm not assuming. I'm willing to get a DNA test."

Mac set the journal back on the desk and eyed his brother.

"Sorry I'm late." Laney swept in, Ryker right on her heels. She tugged her coat off as she glanced between Jack, Mac and Braden. "What did I miss?"

"Here." Braden held out the journal, open to the page that changed Jack's life.

Ryker took the book and read with Laney. Her gasp filled the room, but he just grunted out a laugh.

Ryker took Laney's coat and folded it over the back of a leather chair. "Where did you find this?" he asked.

"He won't say," Mac stated.

Jack wasn't about to let the power slip through his fingers. "Where I found it doesn't matter. Is that Patrick's writing?"

Laney nodded. "Yes. How do we know you're the son he's talking about?"

She eased down into the seat and leaned against her coat, her hand covering her swollen abdomen. "All this time Dad knew he had another child out there and didn't say a word," she murmured. "I bet that tore him up inside."

Jack gritted his teeth. He didn't care what it did to the old bastard. The man was a crooked liar. He'd done vile things to innocent people.

"Your eyes," Laney stated, looking back up at Jack.

He nodded. The eyes clearly told the truth. Everyone in this room, save for Ryker, had the same shade of green eyes.

"That doesn't mean a thing," Ryker snarled. "If you're trying to get money—"

Jack laughed. "Don't be absurd. I couldn't care less about your money. I'm here for the truth."

"You're here with a new approach to try to pin a crime on us we didn't commit," Braden stated.

Jack shrugged. "I could use this information to my favor if I wanted. But I'm starting to believe you."

All eyes turned to him. Yeah, the revelation was just as shocking to him as it was to them. He didn't want to admit he was wrong—who did? But he wasn't going to make excuses for his actions. He'd gone on his instincts and past scenarios, and believed he was working the right angle.

"This is all too coincidental." Mac rose to his full height, crossing his arms over his chest. "Suddenly our long-lost brother comes in and wants to help us save the day against the big, bad Feds."

Jack's cell vibrated in his pocket. Nothing was as important as this, so he ignored it. Again, he was putting his personal life ahead of work.

"I didn't say I believe you completely," he retorted. "I'm willing to work together, and if that clears your name, then so be it."

"What exactly do you want from this meeting?" Braden asked, narrowing his eyes and leaning back in his chair. "You expect us to welcome you to family gatherings or reveal our deepest secrets?"

Jack glanced around the room. Ryker and Mac seemed to be angry, Braden still skeptical, while Laney looked at him as if she wanted to reach out and hug him, but was afraid. So many mixed emotions, so many lies swirling between them, and Jack was trying to set straight as many as he possibly could.

"I don't expect to be trusted, by any means," he stated, glancing back at Braden. "I wouldn't believe me if I were in your shoes. I wanted to present you with what I'd found. The journal is yours to keep. I made copies."

Braden closed the book and tapped his fingers on the leather cover. "I'd still be interested in knowing how this fell into your hands."

The same way everything else lately had fallen into his hands...by chance. Viv had entered his life when he hadn't been looking, just like the journal.

"I have a large reach," he replied. "Same as you. I doubt you give up your informants."

There was no way he'd ever give up Viv's name. No matter what happened between them on a personal level, Jack cared for her, and he'd never want to see her hurt. She'd come to work for him when she'd needed a job, and he'd thrown her into the lion's den. She'd never complained, but had stuck by his side and worked double duty.

And when she'd discovered a journal that uncovered a lie over three decades old, she'd panicked. Jack would be a jerk not to realize that she'd been scared, that she'd been trying to protect him while he finished this case. She knew the amount of time and mental effort he'd put into seeking justice.

And as furious and hurt as he was that she'd kept something so pivotal from him, he'd have to be blind not to see her reasoning.

"You don't have to give up your informant," Braden stated, shifting Jack's focus back to the present. "I know you and Viv have been working together. I've known for some time."

Keeping his cool, refusing to show any sign of affirmation, Jack merely asked, "And what makes you think this?"

Braden shrugged and came to his feet. "She's the likely candidate, but Laney didn't want to believe Viv would turn on us. She's the only reason we kept Viv here."

Jack flashed Laney a glance. The sadness in her eyes proved how much this family had come to care for Viv. Damn it, this was a debacle of epic proportions, because he, too, cared for her. Too much.

"Leave Viv out of this," Jack stated. There was no reason to try to hide the facts or treat them like fools. "She worked for me, but she's no longer in my employment."

"Relax," Mac interjected. "We also kept her here because we have nothing to hide. We know the Feds want to pin the Parkers' tragedy on us. If you want to stop snooping around and actually work together, maybe we can find the guilty parties and clear our name."

Jack tried to process everything happening. First and foremost, Viv's true identity had been discovered long ago and they'd still kept her on. They could've done anything to her, given the rumors surrounding the family. But now that Jack was getting a glimpse inside their lives, inside Patrick's journal, he was starting to see that maybe this family wasn't all death and destruction.

"So you're agreeing to work together?" he asked, taken aback.

"The truth goes both ways," Braden said. "We don't trust easily, but if you want to do this, then we're all-in."

Jack needed Viv, he realized. She had ties to this family that he didn't, and they obviously respected her.

Damn it, that wasn't the only reason he needed her. He missed her, and it had been only hours since he'd seen her, touched her.

But the O'Sheas wanted to work together to clear their name. Jack wanted justice for the Parkers...justice he'd never been able to deliver on behalf of his wife and unborn child.

His family.

And he might have another chance at a family yet. Viv had made a mistake, but she wasn't malicious.

"I'd say with our combined resources, we can solve this case together," Jack agreed. He had to focus on this moment, and deal with his personal life later.

"Get that DNA test," Braden demanded. "I see it, though. I know the truth just by looking at you. What my father wrote may be shocking, but it's the truth. Eyes aside, you've got the O'Shea attitude."

Jack didn't want to have the O'Shea name tacked on to his life. In his line of work, he couldn't afford it. But at the same time, he wanted a family of his own. Only time would tell if this group would be his or not. He wasn't quite ready to cozy up to the idea of holiday dinners or family portraits.

"I'll have it done, but the result stays inside this room." He glanced around at the people who were family by biology...nothing more. "I have a business, a reputation to protect."

Braden smirked. "Can't be associated with the notorious family? I get it. No problem."

Mac glanced at his watch. "I need to pick Jenna up at the airport. She caught an early-morning flight."

Braden nodded. "Go ahead. We'll discuss a game plan and I'll fill you in later."

Once Mac stepped out, Jack and Braden sat down at the desk. He wanted to solve this damn case the FBI had entrusted him with. His priorities had shifted, but he was still keeping his guard up, as he suspected Braden was, too.

"I'm going to go out front and get the store ready to open," Laney stated. "I'll keep this door shut for privacy."

Ryker pulled up a chair beside Braden, his dark eyes narrowing in on Jack. "You need to talk to Viv before we get started?"

Jack shook his head. "No. She has nothing to do with this anymore." But even as he said the words, he knew they weren't true.

"I don't know what's going on between the two of you, but—"

"No, you don't." Jack settled back in his chair as he cut off Braden's words. "Now, let's get to work."

Jack pushed Viv out of his mind so he could concentrate on this all-important meeting.

Too bad he couldn't push her out of his heart.

# Eighteen

Martha was all too eager to watch Katie for the evening, but Viv assured her she wouldn't be long. Valentine's Day sucked, and heading to Jack's house was just salt in the wound. But she had things that needed to be said. Once she got all this off her chest, maybe…

No. She wouldn't feel any better. She'd still feel empty inside, but she had to tell him how she felt and had to defend herself. Added to that, she needed to return all these presents.

She'd piled the ridiculous toys he'd bought into her car. Where on earth would she house a tiny sports car, anyway? Katie didn't need such extravagant gifts and Viv was doing her best to cut all ties with Jack. That was what he'd wanted, after all.

He'd made it perfectly clear that she was of no use to him any longer. But she knew he still cared for her. He wouldn't be so hurt if he didn't care. Plus, she'd seen the way he looked at her, felt how perfectly he'd touched her. They shared a bond whether he wanted it or not. Viv just wished that was enough to get them back where they needed to be. She'd give anything to be able to turn back the clock and hand him that journal the second she'd discovered it.

But she'd made the best decision at the time. At least she thought she had. Hindsight and all that.

Viv pulled in a breath as she tugged her coat tighter around her neck. The snow would not let up. This would be a great night for all those lovers to stay indoors.

She cursed Valentine's Day again as she rang the bell at Jack's Beacon Hill home.

In moments, the wide door swung open and Tilly greeted her with a smile. "Honey, come on in. It's freezing out there."

Viv stepped into the foyer, forcing herself not to look around the house for the man she'd dreamed about all night. She needed to drop the toys off and leave. That's all. Now that she was here in his domain, she couldn't talk to him. What would be the point? He was so furious with her. He hadn't spoken to her or reached out to her at all since he'd left her bed.

"I can't stay," Viv informed Tilly. She needed to get out of here. "I have some things in my car that belong to Jack."

Tilly's brows rose. "Oh, well. I'll go get him—"

"No!" Viv didn't mean to shout, but she didn't want to make this evening any more unbearable than necessary. "I mean, I can carry them in."

Tilly tipped her head to the side, reaching out to grab Viv's hands. Her warm touch threatened to break Viv. She was already so close to an emotional breakdown…she just didn't have time for one.

"I don't know what happened with you guys," Tilly started. "But he's a grouchy bear. I can't get him to eat. He stays in his office and only asks me to bring him more bourbon. I've seen him like this just one other time."

*When his wife died.* The words hovered in the air as if she'd said them.

Viv swallowed the tears clogging her throat. "It's all my fault," she whispered.

"I'm sure it can be fixed." The elderly woman wrapped her arm around Viv and squeezed. "Go talk to him."

Viv shook her head. "He's angry, and rightfully so. I just think it's best if I drop off all these things and be on my way."

Tilly eased back and patted Viv's hands. "His wife was taken from him too soon. You're the first woman I've ever seen him interested in since that time. Are you sure you want to throw all of that away because you're afraid?"

Viv closed her eyes. Was she willing to risk more humiliation and rejection?

"He's upstairs in his study." Tilly took a step back

and gestured toward the grand stairway. "I'll be finishing up in the kitchen before I go. You can bring the toys into the foyer and take off, or you can do what you know in your heart is the right thing. Either way, I'll be leaving shortly."

Tilly headed down the hall to the kitchen.

Viv's chest was heavy as she eyed the steps. She'd never been upstairs, but she wasn't going to let this moment pass her by. She'd say her piece, put the ball in his court, then be gone.

If he truly wanted to sever all ties, then at least she'd know she'd done her part.

Viv gripped the carved newel post and willed her legs to carry her up the steps. Nerves threatened to take over, to force her to turn back around and get out. But Jack was facing one of the most difficult situations of his life and he was justified in his feelings toward her. She couldn't apologize enough, but she wasn't going to miss the chance to say it one last time.

The wide hallway was dark, except for the dim light shining beneath one closed door. Viv pulled in a shaky breath and crossed the distance. She tapped lightly on the door with her knuckles.

"Go away, Tilly. I'm fine."

He didn't sound fine. He sounded…crushed.

Viv didn't knock again, but merely turned the knob and pushed the door open. He was already angry at her. Barging in on his personal space was nothing compared to what she'd done.

"Tilly, I…"

He glanced up from behind his desk, the words dying on his lips as he met her gaze across the room. Viv's heart beat heavily against her chest. She clutched the knob for support as she remained frozen in place.

"I came by to return the toys," she stated. "I, um, well, Tilly said you were up here and…"

The way he sat unmoving, without saying a word, had her nerves spiraling out of control. But she'd come this far and she was going to get this out.

"I know you hate me." She eased forward, one slow step at a time, across the expansive office. "You have every right and I don't blame you. But when I found that journal, I was stunned. My immediate thought was to get it straight to you, but then I realized what that truth would do to you. You think of nothing but justice. When I learned about your wife and child, I understood how deep your need for justice went. You've been trying to bring the O'Sheas down for so long and I didn't want to be the one to crush you."

Motionless, Jack stared at her. The bottle of bourbon sat on the corner of his desk, and he clutched an empty tumbler in his hand. Was he drunk? Was he even listening?

"I kept it hidden, waiting for the right time, hoping the case would wrap up and I could present it to you. I wanted you to be able to separate work from this bombshell because I knew the case was so important."

She stopped at his desk. Tugging the tie on her

coat a little tighter, she wished she had something else to do with her shaky hands. Those green eyes held her in place, pinning her with an unreadable expression.

"But then the timing didn't matter," she went on, biting her bottom lip to prevent the trembling. She attempted to tamp down the tears, but her eyes filled. "I started falling for you. The attraction I'd had for so long turned into something I didn't expect."

Jack came to his feet, setting his glass aside. "Viv—"

"No, let me get this out, then I'll go."

She didn't want him to kick her out, not until she explained herself and apologized the proper way.

"When my feelings got stronger, I cursed the day I found that journal. I didn't want to know that truth, didn't want to carry it around with me, to hold such a burden. I knew it would hurt you no matter when I told you. But I didn't want to be that person, Jack. I didn't want to be the one who had to drop this bomb into your life."

Viv swiped at the tear that slid down her cheek. "I'm sorry I lied. I'm sorry I kept something so vital from you. But at the time, I thought I was doing the right thing by saving you heartache."

Viv took a step back, blinking the moisture from her eyes. "I'm sorry," she whispered. "That's…that's all I wanted to say."

She spun on her heel, more than ready to get out of this room, this house. The ache of seeing him again spread through her and she had no idea how the hell she was going to recover, but she had no choice. She would get through this, in time…she hoped. A little girl was depending on her.

Firm hands gripped her, hauling her back against his chest. "Don't go."

Viv's heart slammed against her chest. "I can't stay, Jack. I've said all I need to say."

He spun her around to face him. The intensity of his gaze had never been so powerful, so raw.

"Well, I haven't said all I need to, and you're going to listen."

She nodded. He deserved to say whatever he wanted, and the hell he was about to throw at her was completely justified.

Jack stepped aside and pointed to the chaise in front of the wall of books. On any other day, she'd marvel at the entire wall of hardbacks, but since she would never be here again, she'd have to just commit the scene to memory.

"Sit down."

Viv shouldn't have been surprised at his aggressive tone, but, well…she was. Without a word, she crossed and took a seat, sliding her fingers along the velvety arm of the chair.

"I've thought about nothing else since I saw that journal," he began, pacing like a caged animal. "My father was a criminal, I've been working to destroy my half siblings, only to find they are legit, and the woman I trusted most lied to my face."

Viv glanced down to the ends of her coat ties. She toyed with a single dangling thread.

"No, you don't get to look away."

She glanced up to find him standing before her. Hands on his hips, he glared down at her.

"You came to me. Now you're going to listen."

She glanced at the bottle on his desk. "How much have you had to drink?" she asked.

Jack snorted. "Not enough to dull the pain, but I'm not drunk."

Viv bit her lips, nerves dancing in her belly, because she had no clue what he was about to tell her. And he was right. She'd come to him, so she would listen.

"Braden and I have come up with a plan and I've gone to the Feds with it. They don't need to know any more than the fact Braden and I are working together. They trust me and they know I'll find the people responsible for this crime."

Viv nodded, glad for that at least. Maybe if he and Braden did this together, Jack would slowly ease into the idea that the O'Sheas weren't monsters.

"That's great," she told him. "I'm happy for you."

He raked a hand over his face and stared up at the ceiling. Only the Tiffany lamp on his desk cast any light in the room. But she saw the pain in his eyes, sensed the frustration rolling off him. She'd hurt him, but he still cared. She felt it.

"I only want what's best for you," she went on. "I know it doesn't seem like that, but I do."

"That's the other thing that has haunted me." He spread his feet wide, crossed his arms and pinned her with that sultry gaze. "I've looked at this from every angle. Mine, yours. I want to push you out of my life for hurting me."

"I understand and I don't blame you." Guilt fueled another round of tears. "I'll just go."

She'd started to stand, when Jack's hands came down on her shoulders and forced her back down.

"You're staying right here." Viv didn't know what to say, especially when Jack squatted down in front of her. "I'm not done talking."

"I get that you're hurting, but we've said everything." She had to get out of here. "Let me unload my car and I'll be out of your life for good."

Jack dropped his head, blew out a breath before looking back up into her eyes. "I don't want you gone, Viv."

Hope slammed into her. "What?"

He reached up and gripped her hands. "I'm upset, yes, but I understand why you did what you did. Hell, I don't know that I'd have done things differently had I been in your position."

Viv blinked, sure she'd heard him wrong.

"When I was torn over what to do about approaching Braden and Mac, I caught a glimpse into what you must have gone through. And that was for people I didn't particularly care about. I know you care about me, so I can only guess how much that tore you up."

Viv pulled her hands from his and stood, causing him to rise, as well. "No. Don't forgive me, Jack. That's not why I'm here. I just—I wanted you to accept my apology. I know we can't go back to where we were. I don't deserve it."

She shoved her hands inside her coat pockets. "I need to get back home."

"Will you just stop?" he demanded, when she started to move past him.

Standing shoulder to shoulder with Jack, she froze, not glancing to her left, where he stood a breath away.

"Damn it, Viv. You love me. Why are you doing this? I'm trying to forgive you. I'm trying to tell you that I'm sorry, too, for thinking the worst. For not listening to your side from the beginning."

Air caught in her lungs as she turned fully toward him. "What?"

"You love me," he said softly, smiling this time. "I know you do or you wouldn't have been so upset about the journal."

She closed her eyes. "You're sorry," she whispered. "I hurt you and you're apologizing. You had every right to—"

He slammed his mouth down onto hers, gripping her wrists at her sides. Jack wasn't gentle, wasn't slow. He consumed her as if he were claiming her all over again. Jack nipped at her lips before easing back to look her in the eyes. "I may not like what you did," he murmured. "But I understand why you did it. And don't bother fighting me or telling me you don't love me, because that won't work at all with my plans."

"What are your plans? To kiss me like you love me, when you know exactly how I feel?"

He laughed, easing her arms behind her back to draw her arched body into his. "Oh, but Viv. I do love you. And that's why I was so hurt."

Viv's heart quickened as she stared up into his eyes. "You what?"

His mouth quirked. "I can admit when I was wrong and I can admit that I love you. I knew I was falling for you, but when I left your apartment, I realized it was love. Someone I didn't care about couldn't get close enough to make it hurt so bad."

Viv closed her eyes. "I never wanted to hurt you. I wanted the exact opposite."

"I know." He nipped at her lips again. "I know you didn't want to hurt me."

Jack pulled back, stared down at her, making her wonder what was going to happen next. Where they would go from here. *He loves me.* The words swirled in her head, her heart. She'd never expected him to return her feelings, never thought he'd forgive her, let alone love her.

"I'm waiting."

Viv narrowed her eyes. "For what?"

He leaned into her, causing her body to arch even further into his. He continued to hold her arms behind her back and Viv ached for his touch, sans clothes.

"For you to tell me you love me. I want the words."

Viv licked her lips, pleased when his eyes watched her mouth. "I love you, Jack. I'm sorry I hurt you. I'm sorry I ever made you doubt my loyalty. But I love you more than I've ever loved anyone in my life."

He started for her mouth again, but Viv turned her head. "Wait."

"What?"

She glanced back. "If you love me, why were you holed up here worrying Tilly to death?"

"I was in a pissy mood about how to approach you," he confessed. "I was coming to your place tomorrow, but I was working through my plan of action to get you back."

Viv raised her brows. "And what was the plan you'd concocted?"

Jack released her hands and immediately went for the tie on her coat. After he peeled the garment off and sent it to the floor, he tugged at the closure on her jeans.

"My plan was to strip you naked, have my way with you and tie you to my bed until you believed me."

Arousal shot through her. "You can still do all those things, but I'm going to have to text Martha first and tell her I'll be a little later than I thought."

Jack gripped the V of her button-up shirt and jerked, sending buttons flying across the room. "I have a feeling she won't mind."

Viv tipped her head back as Jack feasted on her neck, then made his way down to her chest. She'd text Martha…in a bit.

# Epilogue

*One year later...*

"Happy Birthday to you," the whole crew sang.

"Hard to believe she's two already," Jack stated, as Viv helped Katie blow out the two little purple candles on her three-tiered cake. Maybe he'd gone overboard when he ordered the cake, but he did tell Viv she could handle everything else.

"Time flies once you become a parent." Braden held his own baby, Michael, who was six months old now. "I can't believe all the things this little guy is doing on his own already. He's army crawling across the house. Zara went nuts and baby gates are everywhere."

"They're not everywhere," Zara chimed in, sliding a party hat over Braden's head.

"I don't want a hat," he grumbled. "It has a ballerina on it."

"It's not your party," Zara stated, as she patted the side of his face.

"Who wants cake?" Viv announced. "We have plenty and we'll all be eating it for the next week."

She sent Jack a look and a wink. He'd never thought he'd find love again, but everything was different with Viv. She was perfect for him and had come into his life at exactly the right time.

After he'd discovered he was actually an O'Shea, Jack and Braden had worked around the clock to clear their name. It ended up that some wannabe gang members had botched the robbery and tried to cover their tracks. Once Jack had gotten the proper intel, it took only one stakeout to bring down the criminals.

And after all this time, the O'Sheas were completely legit. Braden hadn't been lying; the family had cut ties with all illegal dealings. Their worldwide auction house was more lucrative than ever.

It had taken some time, but Jack and his new siblings were all meshing perfectly together. Jack had wasted no time in marrying Viv and they'd adopted Katie together. They were in the process of adopting another child. He and Viv both wanted a large family and he was more than ready to fill up his large home. Tilly was overjoyed, of course.

As Viv passed out pieces of cake, Katie played with her own layer of purple icing and pink cake.

"More, Mommy." Katie held up her sippy cup with one hand and shoved icing in her mouth with the other.

"I'll get it," Jack said, taking the sticky cup. "You're a messy monster."

Katie smiled at him, her purple teeth flashing. "Wuv you, Daddy."

Those words never failed to make his heart clench. As a man who had thought he'd lost everything, he was beyond blessed with Katie, Viv and the O'Sheas. He literally had every single thing he'd ever wanted at his fingertips.

As he filled Katie's cup with juice, Mac let out a whistle. "While we're all here, I have an announcement."

Jenna stepped close to his side and smiled. Mac wrapped an arm around her, pulling her in tight.

"We're having a baby," he yelled.

Laney squealed, rushing for Jenna and enveloping her in a hug. Ryker stepped up and smacked Mac on the back with one hand, while he held his baby girl on his other arm.

*All these kids...* Jack smiled as he twisted the lid back on the cup. "Looks like there will be a whole new generation of O'Sheas," he proclaimed, crossing back to the dining area. "Just when I thought my house was big enough to host this family..."

"We're going to need a compound if we keep wanting to have family events," Zara said with a laugh. "I'm okay with that, since we plan on having more."

More O'Sheas. At one time that thought would've angered Jack, but now…well, he couldn't be happier.

He threw a glance at Viv, who mouthed, *"I love you."* He sent her a wink and knew he was the luckiest man alive…and that included being an O'Shea.

\* \* \* \* \*

*If you liked this story of a billionaire tamed
by the love of the right woman—and her baby—
pick up these other novels from
Jules Bennett.*

*CAUGHT IN THE SPOTLIGHT
WHATEVER THE PRICE
SNOWBOUND WITH THE BILLIONAIRE
WHAT THE PRINCE WANTS*

*Available now from Harlequin Desire!*

\*\*\*

*And don't miss the next*
**BILLIONAIRES AND BABIES** *story.*
*BILLIONAIRE'S BABY PROMISE
by Sarah M. Anderson.*

*Available March 2017!*

\*\*\*

*If you're on Twitter, tell us what you think
of Harlequin Desire! #harlequindesire*

*If you like sexy and steamy stories with strong heroines and irresistible heroes, you'll love FORGED IN DESIRE by* New York Times *bestselling author Brenda Jackson—featuring Margo Connelly and Lamar "Striker" Jennings, the reformed bad boy who'll do anything to protect her, even if it means lowering the defenses around his own heart...*

*Turn the page for a sneak peek at FORGED IN DESIRE!*

# PROLOGUE

"FINALLY, WE GET to go home."

Margo Connelly was certain the man's words echoed the sentiment they all felt. The last thing she'd expected when reporting for jury duty was to be sequestered during the entire trial…especially with twelve strangers, more than a few of whom had taken the art of bitching to a whole new level.

She was convinced this had been the longest, if not the most miserable, six weeks of her life, as well as a lousy way to start off the new year. They hadn't been allowed to have any inbound or outbound calls, read the newspapers, check any emails, watch television or listen to the radio. The only good thing was, with the vote just taken, a unanimous decision had been reached and justice would be served. The federal case against Murphy Erickson would finally be over and they would be allowed to go home.

"It's time to let the bailiff know we've reached a decision," Nancy Snyder spoke up, interrupting Margo's thoughts. "I have a man waiting at home, who I haven't seen in six weeks, and I can't wait to get to him."

*Lucky you*, Margo thought, leaning back in her

chair. She and Scott Dylan had split over a year ago, and the parting hadn't been pretty.

Fortunately, as a wedding-dress designer, she could work from anywhere and had decided to move back home to Charlottesville. She could be near her uncle Frazier, her father's brother and the man who'd become her guardian when her parents had died in a house fire when she was ten. He was her only living relative and, although they often butted heads, she had missed him while living in New York.

A knock on the door got everyone's attention. The bailiff had arrived. Hopefully, in a few hours it would all be over and the judge would release them. She couldn't wait to get back to running her business. Six weeks had been a long time away. Lucky for her she had finished her last order in time for the bride's Christmas wedding. But she couldn't help wondering how many new orders she might have missed while on jury duty.

The bailiff entered and said, "The judge has called the court back in session for the reading of the verdict. We're ready to escort you there."

Like everyone else in the room, Margo stood. She was ready for the verdict to be read. It was only after this that she could get her life back.

"FOREMAN, HAS THE JURY reached a verdict?" the judge asked.

"Yes, we have, Your Honor."

The courtroom was quiet as the verdict was read. "We, the jury, find Murphy Erickson guilty of murder."

Suddenly Erickson bowled over and laughed. It made the hairs on the necks of everyone in attendance stand up. The outburst prompted the judge to hit his gavel several times. "Order in the courtroom. Counselor, quiet the defendant or he will be found in contempt of court."

"I don't give a damn about any contempt," Erickson snarled loudly. "You!" he said, pointing a finger at the judge. "Along with everyone else in this courtroom, you have just signed your own death warrant. As long as I remain locked up, someone in here will die every seventy-two hours." His gaze didn't miss a single individual.

Pandemonium broke out. The judge pounded his gavel, trying to restore order. Police officers rushed forward to subdue Erickson and haul him away. But the sound of his threats echoed loudly in Margo's ears.

# CHAPTER ONE

LAMAR "STRIKER" JENNINGS walked into the hospital room, stopped and then frowned. "What the hell is he doing working from bed?"

"I asked myself the same thing when I got his call for us to come here," Striker's friend Quasar Patterson said, sitting lazily in a chair with his long legs stretched out in front of him.

"And you might as well take a seat like he told us to do," another friend, Stonewall Courson, suggested, while pointing to an empty chair. "Evidently it will take more than a bullet to slow down Roland."

Roland Summers, CEO of Summers Security Firm, lay in the hospital bed, staring at them. Had it been just last week that the man had been fighting for his life after foiling an attempted carjacking?

"You still look like shit, Roland. Shouldn't you be trying to get some rest instead of calling a meeting?" Striker asked, sliding his tall frame into the chair. He didn't like seeing Roland this way. They'd been friends a long time, and he couldn't ever recall the man being sick. Not even with a cold. Well, at least he was alive. That damn bullet could have taken him out and Striker didn't want to think about that.

"You guys have been keeping up with the news?" Roland asked in a strained voice, interrupting Striker's thoughts.

"We're aware of what's going on, if that's what you want to know," Stonewall answered. "Nobody took Murphy Erickson's threat seriously."

Roland made an attempt to nod his head. "And now?"

"And now people are panicking. Phones at the office have been ringing off the hook. I'm sure every protective security service in town is booked solid. Everyone in the courtroom that day is either in hiding or seeking protection, and with good reason," Quasar piped in to say. "The judge, clerk reporter and bailiff are all dead. All three were gunned down within seventy-two hours of each other."

"The FBI is working closely with local law enforcement, and they figure it's the work of the same assassin," Striker added. "I heard they anticipate he'll go after someone on the jury next."

"Which is why I called the three of you here. There was a woman on the jury who I want protected. It's personal."

"Personal?" Striker asked, lifting a brow. He knew Roland dated off and on, but he'd never been serious with anyone. He was always quick to say that his wife, Becca, had been his one and only love.

"Yes, personal. She's a family member."

The room got quiet. That statement was even more baffling since, as far as the three of them knew, Roland didn't have any family…at least not anymore.

They were all aware of his history. He'd been a cop, who'd discovered some of his fellow officers on the take. Before he could blow the whistle he'd been framed and sent to prison for fifteen years. Becca had refused to accept his fate and worked hard to get him a new trial. He served three years before finally leaving prison but not before the dirty cops murdered Roland's wife. All the cops involved had eventually been brought to justice and charged with the death of Becca Summers, in addition to other crimes.

"You said she's family?" Striker asked, looking confused.

"Yes, although I say that loosely since we've never officially met. I know who she is, but she doesn't know I even exist." Roland then closed his eyes, and Striker knew he had to be in pain.

"Man, you need to rest," Quasar spoke up. "You can cover this with us another time."

Roland's eyes flashed back open. "No, we need to talk now. I need one of you protecting her right away."

Nobody said anything for a minute and then Striker asked, "What relation is she to you, man?"

"My niece. To make a long story short, years ago my mom got involved with a married man. He broke things off when his wife found out about the affair but not before I was conceived. I always knew the identity of my father. I also knew about his other two, older sons, although they didn't know about me. I guess you can say I was the old man's secret.

"One day after I'd left for college, I got a call from

my mother letting me know the old man was dead but he'd left me something in his will."

Striker didn't say anything, thinking that at least Roland's old man had done right by him in the end. To this day, his own poor excuse of a father hadn't even acknowledged his existence. "That's when your two brothers found out about you?" he asked.

"Yes. Their mother found out about me, as well. She turned out to be a real bitch. Even tried blocking what Connelly had left for me in the will. But she couldn't. The old man evidently had anticipated her making such a move and made sure the will was ironclad. He gave me enough to finish college without taking out student loans with a little left over."

"Good for him," Quasar said. "What about your brothers? How did they react to finding out about you?"

"The eldest acted like a dickhead," Roland said without pause. "The other one's reaction was just the opposite. His name was Murdock and he reached out to me afterward. I would hear from him from time to time. He would call to see how I was doing."

Roland didn't say anything for a minute, his face showing he was struggling with strong emotions. "Murdock is the one who gave Becca the money to hire a private investigator to reopen my case. I never got the chance to thank him."

"Why?" Quasar asked.

Roland drew in a deep breath and then said, "Murdock and his wife were killed weeks before my new trial began."

"How did they die?"

"House fire. Fire department claimed faulty wiring. I never believed it but couldn't prove otherwise. Luckily their ten-year-old daughter wasn't home at the time. She'd been attending a sleepover at one of her friends' houses."

"You think those dirty cops took them out, too?" Stonewall asked.

"Yes. While I could link Becca's death to those corrupt cops, there wasn't enough evidence to connect Murdock's and his wife's deaths."

Stonewall nodded. "What happened to the little girl after that?"

"She was raised by the other brother. Since the old lady had died by then, he became her guardian." Roland paused a minute and then added, "He came to see me this morning."

"Who? Your brother? The dickhead?" Quasar asked with a snort.

"Yes," Roland said, and it was obvious he was trying not to grin. "When he walked in here it shocked the hell out of me. Unlike Murdock, he never reached out to me, and I think he even resented Murdock for doing so."

"So what the fuck was his reason for showing up here today?" Stonewall asked. "He'd heard you'd gotten shot and wanted to show some brotherly concern?" It was apparent by Stonewall's tone he didn't believe that was the case.

"Umm, let me guess," Quasar then said languidly. "He had a change of heart, especially now that his niece's life is in danger. Now he wants your help. I assume this is the same niece you want protected."

"Yes, to both. He'd heard I'd gotten shot and claimed he was concerned. Although he's not as much of a dickhead as before, I sensed a little resentment is still there. But not because I'm his father's bastard—a part of me believes he's gotten over that."

"What, then?" Striker asked.

"I think he blames me for Murdock's death. He didn't come out and say that, but he did let me know he was aware of the money Murdock gave Becca to get me a new trial and that he has similar suspicions regarding the cause of their deaths. That's why, when he became his niece's guardian, he sent her out of the country to attend an all-girls school with tight security in London for a few years. He didn't bring her back to the States until after those bad cops were sent to jail."

"So the reason he showed up today was because he thought sending you on a guilt trip would be the only way to get you to protect your niece?" Striker asked angrily. Although Roland had tried hiding it, Striker could clearly see the pain etched in his face whenever he spoke.

"Evidently. I guess it didn't occur to him that making sure she is protected is something I'd want to do. I owe Murdock, although I don't owe Frazier Connelly a damn thing."

"Frazier Connelly?" Quasar said, sitting up straight in his chair. "*The* Frazier Connelly of Connelly Enterprises?"

"One and the same."

Nobody said anything for a while. Then Striker asked, "Your niece—what's her name?"

"Margo. Margo Connelly."

"And she doesn't know anything about you?" Stonewall asked. "Are you still the family's well-kept secret?"

Roland nodded. "Frazier confirmed that today, and I prefer things to stay that way. If I could, I would protect her. I can't, so I need one of you to do it for me. Hopefully, it won't be long before the assassin that Erickson hired is apprehended."

Striker eased out of his chair. Roland, of all people, knew that, in addition to working together, he, Quasar and Stonewall were the best of friends. They looked out for each other and watched each other's back. And if needed they would cover Roland's back, as well. Roland was more than just their employer—he was their close friend, mentor and the voice of reason, even when they really didn't want one. "Stonewall is handling things at the office in your absence, and Quasar is already working a case. That leaves me. Don't worry about a thing, Roland. I've got it covered. Consider it done."

MARGO CONNELLY STARED up at her uncle. "A body-guard? Do you really think that's necessary, Uncle Frazier? I understand extra policemen are patrolling the streets."

"That's not good enough. Why should I trust a bunch of police officers?"

"Why shouldn't you?" she countered, not for the first time wondering what her uncle had against cops.

"I have my reasons, but this isn't about me—this is about you and your safety. I refuse to have you placed in any danger. What's the big deal? You've had a bodyguard before."

Yes, she'd had one before. Right after her parents' deaths, when her uncle had become her guardian. He had shipped her off to London for three years. She'd reckoned he'd been trying to figure out what he, a devout bachelor, was to do with a ten-year-old. When she returned to the United States, Apollo remained her bodyguard. When she turned fourteen, she fought hard for a little personal freedom. But she'd always known the chauffeurs Uncle Frazier hired could do more than drive her to and from school. More than once she'd seen the guns they carried.

"Yes, but that was then and this is now, Uncle Frazier. I can look after myself."

"Haven't you been keeping up with the news?" he snapped. "Three people are dead. All three were in that courtroom with you. Erickson is making sure his threat is carried out."

"And more than likely whoever is committing these murders will be caught before there can be another shooting. I understand the three were killed while they were away from home. I have enough paperwork to catch up on here for a while. I didn't even leave my house today."

"You don't think a paid assassin will find you here? Alone? You either get on board with having a bodyguard or you move back home. It's well secured there."

Margo drew in a deep breath. Back home was the Connelly estate. Yes, it was secure, with its state-of-the-art surveillance system. While growing up, she'd thought of the ten-acre property, surrounded by a tall wrought iron fence and cameras watching her every move, as a prison. Now she couldn't stand the thought of staying there for any long period of time…especially if Liz was still in residence.

Margo's forty-five-year-old uncle had never married and claimed he had his reasons for never wanting to. But that didn't keep him from occasionally having a live-in mistress under his roof. His most recent was Liz Tillman and, as far as Margo was concerned, the woman was a *gold digger*.

"It's final. A bodyguard will be here around the clock to protect you until this madness is over."

Margo didn't say anything. She wondered if at any time it had crossed her uncle's mind that they were at her house, not his, and she was no longer a child but a twenty-six-year-old woman. In a way she knew she should appreciate his concern, but she refused to let anyone order her around.

He was wrong in assuming she hadn't been keeping up with the news. Just because she was trying to maintain a level head didn't mean a part of her wasn't a little worried.

She frowned as she glanced up at him. The last thing she wanted was for him to worry needlessly about her. "I'll give this bodyguard a try…but he better be forewarned not to get underfoot. I have a lot of work to do." She wasn't finished yet. "And another thing, Uncle Frazier," she said, crossing her arms over her chest. "I think you forget sometimes that I'm twenty-six and live on my own. Just because I'm going along with you on this, I hope you don't think you can start bulldozing your way with me."

He glowered at her. "You're stubborn like your father."

She smiled. "I'll take that as a compliment." Dropping her hands, she moved back toward the sofa and sat down, grabbing a magazine off the coffee table to flip through. "So, when do we hire this bodyguard?"

"He's been hired. In fact, I expect him to arrive in a few minutes."

Margo's head jerked up. "What?"

*Find out what happens when Margo and Striker come face-to-face in FORGED IN DESIRE by* New York Times *bestselling author Brenda Jackson.*

*Available February 2017 from Brenda Jackson and HQN Books.*

## #2509 THE TEN-DAY BABY TAKEOVER

*Billionaires and Babies* • by Karen Booth

When Sarah Daltry barges into billionaire Aiden Langford's office with
his secret baby, he strikes a deal—help him out for ten days as the
nanny and he'll help with her new business. Love isn't part of the deal...

## #2510 EXPECTING THE BILLIONAIRE'S BABY

*Texas Cattleman's Club: Blackmail* • by Andrea Laurence

Thirteen years after their breakup, Deacon Chase and Cecelia Morgan
meet again...and now he's her billionaire boss! But while Deacon
unravels the secrets between them, Cecelia discovers she has a little
surprise in store for him, as well...

## #2511 PRIDE AND PREGNANCY

by Sarah M. Anderson

Secretly wealthy FBI agent Tom Yellow Bird always puts the job first. But
whisking sexy Caroline away to his luxury cabin is above and beyond.
And when they end up in bed—and expecting!—it could compromise
the most important case of his career...

## #2512 HIS EX'S WELL-KEPT SECRET

*The Ballantyne Brothers* • by Joss Wood

Their weekend in Milan led to a child, but after an accident, rich jeweler
Jaeger Ballantyne can't remember any of it! Now Piper Mills is back in
his life, asking for his help, and once again he can't resist her...

## #2513 THE MAGNATE'S MAIL-ORDER BRIDE

*The McNeill Magnates* • by Joanne Rock

When a Manhattan billionaire sets his sights on ballerina Sofia Koslov for
a marriage of convenience to cover up an expensive family scandal, will
she gain the freedom she's always craved, or will it cost her everything?

## #2514 A BEAUTY FOR THE BILLIONAIRE

*Accidental Heirs* • by Elizabeth Bevarly

Hogan has inherited a fortune! He's gone from mechanic to billionaire
overnight and can afford to win back the socialite who once broke his
heart. So he hires his ex's favorite chef, Chloe, to lure her in, but soon
he's falling for the wrong woman...

This was a mistake. Jonathan Bear was absolutely certain of it. But he had earned millions making mistakes, so what was one more? Nobody else had responded to his ad.

Except for this pale, strange little creature who looked barely twenty and wore the outfit of an eighty-year-old woman.

She was… Well, she wasn't the kind of formidable woman who could stand up to the rigors of working with him.

His sister, Rebecca, would say—with absolutely no tact at all—that he sucked as a boss. And maybe she was right, but he didn't really care. He was busy, and right now he hated most of what he was busy with.

There was irony in that, he knew. He had worked hard all his life. He had built everything he had, brick by brick. And every brick built a stronger wall against all the things he had left behind. Poverty, uncertainty, the lack of respect.

Finally, Jonathan Bear, that poor Indian kid who wasn't worth anything to anyone, bastard son of the biggest bastard in town, had his house on the side of the mountain and more money than he would ever be able to spend.

And he was bored out of his mind.

Boredom, it turned out, worked him into a hell of a temper. He had a feeling Hayley Thompson wasn't strong enough to stand up to that. But he expected to go through a few assistants before he found one who could handle it. She might as well be number one.

"You've got the job," he said. "You can start tomorrow."

Her eyes widened, and he noticed they were a strange shade of blue. Gray in some lights, shot through with a dark, velvet navy that reminded him of the ocean before a storm. It made him wonder if there was some hidden strength there.

They would both find out.

*Don't miss*
**SEDUCE ME, COWBOY**
*by* New York Times *bestselling author Maisey Yates,*
*available November 2016 wherever*
*Harlequin® Desire books and ebooks are sold.*

www.Harlequin.com

# REQUEST YOUR FREE BOOKS!
## 2 FREE NOVELS PLUS 2 FREE GIFTS!

(H) HARLEQUIN®

*Desire*

## ALWAYS POWERFUL, PASSIONATE AND PROVOCATIVE

**YES!** Please send me 2 FREE Harlequin® Desire novels and my 2 FREE gifts (gifts are worth about $10). After receiving them, if I don't wish to receive any more books, I can return the shipping statement marked "cancel." If I don't cancel, I will receive 6 brand-new novels every month and be billed just $4.55 per book in the U.S. or $5.24 per book in Canada. That's a savings of at least 13% off the cover price! It's quite a bargain! Shipping and handling is just 50¢ per book in the U.S. and 75¢ per book in Canada.* I understand that accepting the 2 free books and gifts places me under no obligation to buy anything. I can always return a shipment and cancel at any time. Even if I never buy another book, the two free books and gifts are mine to keep forever.

225/326 HDN GH2P

Name _____ (PLEASE PRINT)

Address _____ Apt. #

City _____ State/Prov. _____ Zip/Postal Code

Signature (if under 18, a parent or guardian must sign)

### Mail to the **Reader Service:**
**IN U.S.A.:** P.O. Box 1867, Buffalo, NY 14240-1867
**IN CANADA:** P.O. Box 609, Fort Erie, Ontario L2A 5X3

**Want to try two free books from another line?**
**Call 1-800-873-8635 or visit www.ReaderService.com.**

* Terms and prices subject to change without notice. Prices do not include applicable taxes. Sales tax applicable in N.Y. Canadian residents will be charged applicable taxes. Offer not valid in Quebec. This offer is limited to one order per household. Not valid for current subscribers to Harlequin Desire books. All orders subject to credit approval. Credit or debit balances in a customer's account(s) may be offset by any other outstanding balance owed by or to the customer. Please allow 4 to 6 weeks for delivery. Offer available while quantities last.

**Your Privacy**—The Reader Service is committed to protecting your privacy. Our Privacy Policy is available online at www.ReaderService.com or upon request from the Reader Service.

We make a portion of our mailing list available to reputable third parties that offer products we believe may interest you. If you prefer that we not exchange your name with third parties, or if you wish to clarify or modify your communication preferences, please visit us at www.ReaderService.com/consumerchoice or write to us at Reader Service Preference Service, P.O. Box 9062, Buffalo, NY 14240-9062. Include your complete name and address.

HDI5

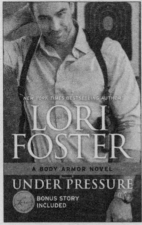